SICK LITTLE PUPPIES

A HORROR SHORT STORY COLLECTION

STEFAN TAYLOR

SIMON J GREEN

Sick Little Puppies
a horror short story collection
by
STEFAN TAYLOR & SIMON J GREEN
Copyright © 2018 by STEFAN TAYLOR & SIMON J GREEN

Cover Design, Layout & Typeset: David Schembri Studios

The authors would like to acknowledge:
Amanda J. Spedding for her power edits and honesty. David Schembri for his vicious cover design and kind style formatting. Clare Pickering and Amra Pajalic for their eagle eyes over our stupid errors. All of them authors, so check them out, too!

Stefan would like to acknowledge:
All the friends and family that smile, nod, and pat me on the back when I tell them what I'm working on at the moment. To SJG, my partner in crime and friend, (I promise to adhere to the three act structure at all times.) Finally, to you, wonderful reader! For taking a chance and giving us a shot. Thank you and enjoy.

Simon would like to acknowledge:
First, my wife Lisa Green, who reads everything but more than that, guards my soul. Stefan Taylor, we made a TV show together 11 years ago and now you're my favourite artist and friend to collaborate with. To the cystic fibrosis teams at the Royal Children's, the Monash and The Alfred in Melbourne, thanks for keeping me alive. To all the film, TV, theatre, graphic design and digital creators I've worked with over the years, and who maintained kind, reciprocal relationships, thank you. Being an artist in Australia is hard, but doing it with grace is harder.

ISBN-978-0-6483281-1-7
www.stefantaylor.com.au
www.simonjgreen.com

Published by The X Gene Pty Ltd
Melbourne, Australia

SICK
LITTLE
PUPPIES

CONTENTS

In the Grip of Shadows

By Stefan Taylor

The familiar surroundings had comforted him at first. The large house where he'd grown up was filled with memories. Every scratch on the walls or stain on the carpet told a story. He'd always felt safe here. The house was more than his home. It was his sanctuary.

But things were different now. The walls seemed to shimmer and bend when he passed, and the sun didn't blaze as brightly through the windows as it used to. A strange veil had fallen over his vision, as if everything was a dream from which he could not wake.

He wondered if other dead people saw it the same.

While he could move through his home, uninhibited by walls and doors, he could not leave the house.

He'd tried everything to make his family aware of him.

He was here, he was with them, but they couldn't see. He tried banging on the walls, moving small objects—all of which was incredibly taxing on his strength. He'd even screamed right into his mother's face, but his cry was lost between the worlds of the living and the dead.

His passing had destroyed his parents' already broken relationship. The nights had become a downward spiral of arguments and tears as they raged at each other with so much venom.

One night, when the walls had ceased reverberating with the sounds of his parents' battle, he'd been shattered to find his sister, Wendy, crouching behind the sofa, tears streaming down her pale face. He'd wanted to comfort her, to wipe the tears away, but his touch was nothing more than a chill in the air.

Was this his hell? Was his punishment to watch those he loved destroy each other, bit by bit? But what could he do? They had no idea he was with them. He was just a memory now; a face in fading photographs that hung on walls, or sat in dusty photo albums. So, he walked unseen down the dark corridors of the cavernous house, or floated over his family's beds, watching the soft rise and fall of their chests as they slept. Sometimes, when he felt truly desolate, he would fly up to a shadowed corner of the large attic. There he would curl up and hope to fight off the ever-growing loneliness.

"James," he would whisper to himself. "My name is James." He hoped he would not forget.

It was as the last dim rays of twilight were being smothered by night, that James first saw them. He had been in his sister's room watching the setting sun through her large bay window when out of the corner of his eye, a tall, dark shape…almost like a shadow, stepped through the doorway.

At least, it looked like a shadow, with its fuzzy outlines and dark centre, but there was nothing near the doorway to cast the shadow.

The thing was too big to be human, and it seemed to twitch and jerk slightly, swaying in the doorway. The thing had no eyes that he could discern, yet James could feel it inspecting him. Suddenly, it slipped out of the room, a gust of cool air raced after it.

Before he knew what he was doing, James shot out into the hall in search of the spectre. He hurried down the long hallway to his dad's study. "Wait!" he called after it. "Please!"

The door to his father's study was wide open, the curtains drawn. The room was silent except for the methodical *tick, tick, tick* of the old clock on the mantle.

"I just want to talk to you. Can you see me?" James listened. Maybe he'd imagined the shadowy thing. "Is anyone there?"

A loud grunt sounded from the far corner. Something *was* here.

For long moments he stared into the dark. Something began to shift in the far corner, pulling itself from the shadows. It groaned and twitched, like an animal in its final death throes.

James backed away, but the thing kept coming.

A long, gossamer arm snapped out and brushed his face sending a biting chill through his whole being.

He fled the room, the walls a blur as he rushed past. He

hurried up to his place in the attic and it was only much later, when he heard the familiar din of his parents' battle, that he dared descend. James cautiously checked the dark corners of the house, but found no sign of the shadow.

Still shaken by his encounter, he again retreated to the attic, unaware of the things that watched him as he passed.

At midnight they appeared.

Three hulking shadows whose forms constantly shifted and changed. They moved slowly and purposely, gliding through the house. In the hall, the shadows were still, enjoying the sensations of this new home. Yes, this would do nicely. Here they could feed.

The spirit boy was a bonus, so much fear in him, so much to consume. The largest of the three stretched to its full height, its head almost touching the ceiling. It looked down at the other two, who shrank back like frightened puppies. Unspoken words passed between them and they silently dispersed.

The smallest shadow slithered into the girl-child's room. There it gleefully whispered into her ear, filling her slumber with hideous dreams she could never have imagined.

The second shadow slid into the mother's room, where it wrapped her in its cloak of misery. The woman twitched and turned as the shadow embraced her with its darkness.

The largest of the shadows hung from the light fitting observing the man who lay fully clothed on the couch. There was plenty the shadow could do with this, but what would yield the best results? Ah, of course. Hate. Hate always led to anger, and anger to violence. It just had to plant the right seeds. It lowered itself to the man's ear and began to whisper lies and deceptions. The man's hands began to clench in his sleep, his jaw bulging at the falsehoods.

And as the night continued its slow crawl towards dawn, the shadows continued to feed.

For many nights, James watched the shadows as they continued to feed. He could do nothing as his family disintegrated. Over the following weeks his sister became a mute, even when their father was standing over her, roaring at her to speak. His mother wept, or sat staring out the window, defeated and broken. And his father was nothing short of a monster.

Every night when his father got home, he raged at the family. James had even seen him kick a hole through the wall in the kitchen and smash his fist against the bathroom mirror, shattering it.

And always the shadows lurked in the background, feeding and growing stronger.

It was only during the day when the family was out, that the shadows would retreat to the dim corners of the house and wait.

Even then he could sense them watching him. He didn't dare leave his place in the attic, his new prison within his old one. He had to do something! But what could beat these creatures of the dark? A thought crept up on him. There was only one thing that could drown out the dark. At least he hoped it could.

There was only one way to find out.

Late one evening, James cautiously floated down to the hallway.

He could feel the shadows' presence – they were busy feeding. He had a plan. Whether it worked or not, was another matter.

He hung back and waited until he saw the pale rays of morning through the hall windows. James made for Wendy's room, keeping close to the wall, wary of the shadows cast by the now-waning moon. There it was, crouched by her bed, its hunched form looking solid now. It was whispering in guttural tones, and although James couldn't quite make out the words, strange, nightmarish images flashed before him. So vivid that he felt himself falter.

Pieces of the shadow's dreams hissed and danced in his mind, dreams that it was pouring unrelentingly into the fragile soul of his sister.

Fury overcame his fear, and he shot out from the darkness, pouncing on the black terror. It was like hitting a wall of ice.

The shadow twisted awkwardly against him. It seemed surprised by the unexpected attack, but it quickly overcame the shock. He felt its entire rage forced on him, its chilling presence driving him into the dark.

James wrapped himself around the icy form and tried to hold the writhing creature. "Leave her alone!" he screamed in his mind. The shadow's featureless face twisted to the side. *It heard! It can understand!*

"Leave her alone!"

The shadow rolled and contorted and suddenly it was free of his grip. Its icy touch hit him in his very being, and he found himself pinned. The images it had been feeding into Wendy's mind were now in his, as clear as real life. He could feel his sanity beginning to falter under the onslaught. But the light of day was beginning to drown out the dark. Now was the moment.

With all that he was, James wrapped himself tightly around the shadow, wrapping himself tightly around it as it began to thrash.

He pulled it, inch by painful inch, into the light.

The shadow howled its fear and rage, and tried to pull itself back to the safety of the dark. James could feel the creature's icy touch clawing at him, but still he held fast. *Just a little longer. Just a little longer.*

Finally, the sun peeked over the horizon and bathed the room in its warmth. The shadow screamed and flapped in James' grip until he could hold it no more. He watched as it crawled like a wounded animal for the safety of the dark and vanished. He had not succeeded in killing the thing, but it was clear he had dealt it a crippling blow.

He sprawled in the morning sun and contemplated his chances in the war that was now certain to come.

There was no feeding that night, just the feeling of dark energies turning their attention to the attic.

They found him huddled in his corner, and hovered there for what seemed an age, as if they had not decided exactly what to do.

Their anger was palpable; a solid, weighty thing that pinned him in place, but he had nowhere to run, so he waited. Finally, the larger of the remaining two moved forward. The whole attic blackened and then, to his horror, it spoke.

The voice was a sick parody of a human speech, cracked and

gruff. The thing's tones were so deep that he felt its words.

"Do… you know… what… we are?" it growled.

He didn't dare reply.

"We… once lived in the light… no more… cast to dark… we are the dark now, we follow… suffering," the shadow seemed to inhale, as if struggling with the act of speech.

"We come to feed… must always feed… *will* always feed." It wheezed and moved closer. "We… can hurt you… even in death… can hurt… see? See!"

An icy wind whipped about them. James felt the solid floor disintegrate beneath him, replaced by a whirling, yawning pit. He heard distant cries and screams, and felt a clammy, withered thing slide around his being.

Frantically he tried to squirm free. Strange pains hit him from all angles, as if he were flesh again. He felt the sickening sensation of his limbs being torn from their sockets. He howled his agony in the dark; the cries from below became louder as if in response.

Then it stopped. It was just him and the shadows once more.

"See?" the shadow growled. "See our… home? We… escaped… you won't."

Somehow they had changed locations and were now in the living room. He must've been pulled toward the pit. "If you hurt my family I'll… I'll—"

Both shadows grunted and groaned with laughter, the sound piercing the stillness. The large shadow encircled James with its icy energy. "You… you… brought us here… opened the door… *you.*"

He had brought them? How?

"My family won't survive," James whispered.

"No…but…maybe they join you…happy family…together…again." The shadow turned its massive head and hissed.

James had defeated one shadow, but these two were fearfully strong, and his being was still reeling from his brief experience with the abyss.

"Go… back to your… your hidden… place… or… we feed… on you." The shadow's voice was beginning to falter; it was clearly using a lot of power just by speaking.

If James was going to do anything, it had to be now.

He lashed out with a howl of defiance; the large shadow was driven back but not far. They were so strong! Their two forms combined and swirled around him. Terror gripped him as the dark abyss yawned opened again. One of the shadows drew him close to its sunken, blank face.

"This…your home… now," it growled.

James was being forced down towards the abyss. The distant howls of those who had gone before could be heard in the deep. With every last bit of his will he hauled himself to the edge and hung there. He knew, however, that he was only delaying the inevitable.

Suddenly, from the corner of his eye, a small figure peered around the door to the living room. Wendy was looking in. No, not just looking in, she was staring right at him! Could she see him?

Her face uncertain, frightened, and although he had never really paid much care to her in his teen years, he knew he couldn't leave her to the mercy of the shadows.

As swiftly as he could, James wrapped his shredded being around the creatures and dragged them to him. At the same time he released his grip on the edge of the abyss. The three spectres plunged toward the screams and howls below.

The shadows tried desperately to free themselves from his grip, but already they knew it was too late. They were coming home, falling back toward the icy depths they'd spent eons trying to escape.

James simply let himself fall and braced himself for an eternity in the darkness.

In his mind he held on to the knowledge that his one last act of sacrifice had freed the ones he loved from the grip of the shadows.

He smiled his last smile, and then he hit the frozen dark.

The screams were deafening.

In the quiet of the living room, Wendy stood looking at the spot where only moments ago, dark shadows had writhed and twisted before her. It seemed they were gone now. She felt lighter, her mind clear.

It was as if a great weight had been lifted from the whole house. She breathed, and padded back down the hall to her bedroom and her first peaceful sleep in months.

***

Jill watched from the large bay window as her daughter ran laughing around the backyard. Her husband playfully pursued the child, caught her and began tickling her. He looked up and smiled. She smiled back. The child rolled away and the pursuit started again. She folded the last of the laundry and laid it neatly on the bed.

It was now twelve months since her son, James, had taken his own life. The image of him swinging in the corner of the attic still woke her at night, and she knew that it would haunt her until her dying day. She'd always known her son was having problems, but never had she thought he would… harm himself. If it hadn't been for her daughter, the guilt might have claimed her too.

She pushed the thought aside.

Things had been looking up recently. Her husband had returned to his old self, and her daughter was not only talking again, but never shut up.

And there was part of her that could still feel James' presence in the house.

She hadn't said anything to her husband of course, but there was definitely something that walked the hallway at night, looking in at them. At first she had been frightened but now it seemed normal.

She smiled; it *was* James, watching over them. In fact, even now she could feel something in the room with her. She held her breath and listened, a few creaks from the corner behind her and a cool gust of air. Yes, James was still with them.

She jumped as loud banging resounded from the window.

"Mum, come outside with us," Wendy yelled.

"Ok, I'll be right out."

Jill stood and walked to the door, pausing to look around once more before she closed it.

The room was silent. From a high, dark corner, the small

shadow settled down to wait for nightfall. It had taken a long time to rebuild its strength after the battle with the spirit boy. But now felt stronger than ever.

Yes, the time was right to feed again.

Rough Deal

By Simon J Green

First published at Snap Journal http://snapjournal.com.au

Larissa was polite. As a marketing manager working with external suppliers, she needed open body language, and an even, patient tone when allowing Marcus to put forward his ideas. Larissa was perfectly cordial when she shot down those ideas and suggested her own. By insisting, even after he offered his adverse opinion, that "Maybe we should give it a try anyway?" she was making sure the firm got what it needed. Larissa was surprised when, after the fifth idea she'd neatly cast aside, the architect snapped back.

"Look, I really don't understand why you're here." Marcus frowned, shifting away from the plans on the table so he was facing her fully. The booth seating brought them uncomfortably close. "You've clearly got an idea in your head. What's the point in having this conversation?"

Larissa's eyebrows raised, her mouth opened slightly as she feigned emotion. "There's no need for that," she explained, patiently, politely. "This is a collaborative process, isn't it?"

Marcus's eyes narrowed; he'd heard that phrase from his client so many times it had lost all meaning. He was terrible at hiding his reactions. "It's supposed to be, yes."

She could read his every shift. Ignoring the sarcasm, she pushed on. "Then we just want to make sure we're getting what we need. We're making a large investment in this."

"Sure, but I'd rather the thing be..." he trailed off, thought about his next words. "I'd rather we be in sync with what you need and what my expertise is telling me."

Larissa leaned in to her supplier. "Look, I know," she agreed. "I have to keep my boss happy. You know what it's like. He doesn't always get this sort of stuff straight away. We have to walk him through it."

Marcus's frown deepened. He opened his mouth to speak, but closed it, looking down at the papers. "OK." He lifted one of the plans. "What would *your boss* do here?"

She glanced at the contentious section of blueprint and reinforced what she'd been seeking the whole time. "I've already said – sorry, my boss has already said we need it bigger and wider."

Marcus's body suddenly loosened. His tension melted into the booth. He took a sip of his drink, then smiled at her, looking directly into her eyes. "Sure," his voice was lower, soothing. "Your boss is right. Bigger and wider. Let's do that."

As she proceeded to divulge all the ideas she'd had for this new building, Larissa marvelled at how being polite always worked for her, eventually.

When they'd finished, the sun was setting. Larissa rolled up her files and plans, and enquired why Marcus wasn't doing the same.

"I'll have another drink and take some notes." He smiled that same relaxed smile. Was he tipsy?

As she headed for the door, she heard him call for the waiter. *Numbing his wounds.* Creatives could be so petty. This was just business. A transaction.

She left the restaurant then headed to the lobby. As she waited for the lift, she opened a corner of the plans and peeked in at the features she'd added. A small thrill raced up her spine. This was going to be her masterpiece. Getting some of it over the line with her boss was the next challenge. She could use Marcus's intransigence, by plucking complaints he'd made about her suggestions and reconfigure them to baffle the boss into submission. The *ding* of the lift broke her from her reverie.

In the restaurant, the waitress returned with a 24-year-old scotch. Marcus was rising as she placed it on the table. "Thanks… is it Shirley?" She nodded. "Just leave it here for a tick," he said as he threw on his jacket. "I'll be back, just doing some maintenance." Shirley went back to the chef in the kitchen and asked her boss why the maintenance man was able to order such an expensive scotch. The chef laughed and sliced a fish in two. "That's the architect who built this place, Shirl." Shirley blushed and thought back over whether she'd said anything stupid.

<hr>

Larissa waited as a young, scruffy person got out of the lift. Another classless creative sauntering to work late. She couldn't wait to be out of this building. Marcus was a talented enough architect to have designed the place from the ground up to accommodate his business, but it lacked something she thought crucial: exclusivity. Larissa stepped into the lift daydreaming about all the riff raff they could deny entry to at their new headquarters. First would be Marcus, once he'd done all they'd asked of him.

As the lift neared garage parking, Larissa just wanted to get to her BMW and get out of here. The lift slipped past B1… B2… then down further. The last button on the panel said B4, yet still the lift kept descending.

Larissa glanced at the lit numbers above the door, then tapped the open button, then tapped her level again. *Dammit!* She moved her hand toward the emergency stop button when suddenly the lift bobbed to a standstill and the doors slid open.

With the plans held tight to her chest, Larissa poked her head out past the doors. It was a parking level, but it was completely empty. Thick concrete columns stood in perfect rows, supporting the grey ceiling above parking bays. Fluorescent strips, like every other carpark, saturated the yawning space in sickly light. There was no one and nothing to be lit.

Larissa pulled back into the lift and pressed the button for her level again. Nothing happened. She stabbed frantically, impotently. A sudden fury swept through her. She stormed from the lift to find the stairwell that would take her out.

She looked left and right, trying to find the exits and feeling foolish. She heard the grinding of the lift doors, then the soft groan as it hoisted itself back up. She ran around to the other side of the lift shaft to see if there were stairs. Her heels clicked as she rounded the corner.

All she found was more carpark with empty bays stretching back so far, she struggled to make out the perimeters. A few presses of the lift's call button accomplished nothing.

Sweat prickled the back of her neck. She dabbed at it with her sleeve and determined she should find those emergency stairs. The snap of her heels echoed through the empty space as she strode forward.

"His precious little building's broken," she muttered, louder than necessary, her words giving her comfort in the bright loneliness.

She scanned her surrounds constantly, hoping to see the walls, and confused by the breadth of the place. It far exceeded the tower above.

A movement. Something fluttering behind a column.

"Thank Christ… HELLO?"

No response.

Walking at a clip now, she closed on the column then rounded to find more bitumen. Frowning, Larissa called out again; a little softer this time.

"Hello?"

A heavy bang caused her to jolt. She spun to the sound.

In the far distance, light after light switched off. One by one, each row of lights died with a heavy thud, as if a giant were stomping across the level above, storming toward her. As great channels of power were suddenly cut, a wall of thick black sped closer in surges.

Though it was only darkness, panic wrapped itself around her. Larissa turned and ran. Each thud became louder, closer, as she fled. She kicked off her heels, glancing behind to see the grip of night choke another row of columns.

It was closing in on her.

Fast.

On nylon covered feet she sprinted, oblivious to what broken and slicing things might be strewn on the tarmac. Her throat was dry, her temples hot, her lungs aching as she struggled to take in more air.

The beat of dying lights gained still. A fresh wave of panic hit. She whimpered.

The thuds suddenly stopped.

The light overhead held, humming gently.

She drew to a stop and leaned against a nearby column, bent over, gasping for air at the edge of darkness. The cessation of rhythm, the sudden silence brought an even eerier sense of unease to the carpark.

Larissa suddenly laughed, a high-pitched sound. Coupled with her exhaustion and the adrenaline dump, her legs gave out and she slid down the column, holding the back of her neck against the cool, painted concrete. What a ridiculous thing! Running from the dark like a little girl! She realised she'd crushed Marcus's plans in her fists, so let them fall to the ground. She looked at her shaking hands and felt embarrassed.

A skittering noise whipped her eyes back to the halted dark. Just beyond the remaining lights was enveloping black. Larissa squinted into the absence of light.

A guttural growl bubbled forth. It sounded like a dog, but the growl was deeper, more menacing, and from something… bigger.

Larissa shot to her feet and hid behind her column. She realised she'd left her paperwork in plain sight. Hiding would be useless when folders and papers sat in an otherwise desolate carpark. Quickly, she reached out and scraped everything toward her. She stole a glance at the darkness.

Something emerged.

It was taller than a man, and while it had two legs they looked odd, bent the wrong way, and they branched up to a broad, powerful torso.

She pulled back from the terror that padded out of shadows, her heart racing. Where was she!? What was happening!? Tears slid down her cheeks as she tried to muffle her sobs, terrified she'd give herself away but struggling for control.

Its footfalls were soft, but in the silence of the space, all too audible. A scrape followed each step. The sounds drew closer, and she closed her mouth tight.

She looked down at her own feet, and realised the rows

of lights cast shadows on the concrete. A much larger shadow, engulfed her own.

The thing paused, sniffed. Then pulled back.

Silence.

She let out a shaky breath.

Had she imagined it? This whole scenario, the exhaustion from sprinting, the lateness of the hour: was she so disoriented she was seeing things? She peeked around the column. Nothing. She felt sick, tired, mentally tortured. And so very angry.

Marcus would receive complaint in every form applicable for getting her trapped down here. She felt a rush of warm air on her arm and turned to the other side of the column.

The wolf's face, fangs bared, eyes of bright yellow, hung over her.

It growled. "Run."

She spun and fled. No path, no plan, just blind fear.

Columns flew past in her periphery. Her feet caught stray pieces of path, puncturing her soles. She felt none of it. All she knew was a predator chasing its prey. And she was the prey.

That primal realisation that she was losing energy and likely to die rebooted her mind. She started weaving between columns, hoping to outwit it, outrun it. Hoping for something. Anything.

From the corner of her eyes, Larissa could see the predator loping around the obstacles. A set of claws screeched across the painted concrete. It pounced, but Larissa ducked around another column. A heavy thud sounded, followed by a yelp. She sprinted off, looked over her shoulder, hopeful, and lost her footing, tumbling into another damn column. Blood burst out of her face. Her breath was knocked from her. She smashed to the ground like a rag doll. Everything went fuzzy.

Her fear vanished as a sweet sensation coursed through her veins. Darkness closed in. She was being rocked, jiggled. Pressure built on her stomach. The pressure grew.

Then she understood.

Then she screamed.

Her screams bounced around the cavernous carpark, but no one could hear her suffering as she was eaten alive.

Soon, there was just tearing and crunching.

In the restaurant, Shirley looked over to Marcus's table. It'd been more than an hour. She walked over and collected his scotch, unsure what to do with it. Not being a scotch drinker, and never of anything so expensive, was it OK to be left out for so long? Just as she turned to ask Chef, Marcus bumped into her. She gasped, and he held her waist to help balance her.

"Woah! Sorry, Shirley, caught you off guard, aye?"

She indicated the drink, "I wasn't sure what to…"

He swiped it and took a gulp, closed his eyes and stood there savouring it. Shirley waited awkwardly. Finally, he slid into the booth and ordered another drink, then asked her to grab a "cheeky one for herself and Chef."

Shirley looked at the collection on the wall, "Something top shelf, too?"

Marcus grinned a toothy grin, "Go for it." Shirley winked and turned, but Marcus caught her one last time. He handed her all the files and notes from the table. "And put these in the bin, would you please?"

"Sure." Shirley frowned for a moment, thinking them too important to rubbish, but not questioning the man plying expensive booze. "Did you want anything for dinner?"

"No thank you," Marcus replied, leaning back in his booth. "I've already eaten."

Homecoming

By Stefan Taylor

It had been three months since her mother's passing, and Sarah could see the old family home was already starting to decay. Weeds had begun invading the floorboards and walls, and there was a thick scent of rotting flowers and stale perfume.

There wasn't much left here. Just memories of a childhood filled with strange visitors, of late night revels she never really understood. She could still hear the local boys from town chanting, "Old bitch" and "Crazy witch" before hurling rocks at the house then bolting back into the surrounding bush.

When she was old enough, Sarah had gotten as far from home as possible, but her mother had always said, *"One day you'll come back, darling. We all come home eventually."*

Sarah's husband had finished clearing the house of its

clutter, and had driven back to the city, leaving her to salvage any keepsake left in the rustic dwelling. However, apart from tins of expired food and her mother's crumbling books, there was nothing of real worth.

Well, there was the painting.

It took all her willpower to turn to the wall and look at it. She knew it well enough. All her life it had hung in that spot, its creator long forgotten.

Her mother had doted on the painting, spent hours admiring it, almost in a trance. Age had faded the image to a dry and flaky ruin. The painting was of the front of the house, only it looked a lot fresher than it did now. On the porch an elderly looking woman was leaning against one of the posts, her hand raised as if waving. At the bottom of the frame was a rusted plaque with the words 'Homecoming' etched in stately writing.

The only thing unnerving about the scene, was the face of the old woman. Whether through the artist's design, or the fading of time, the woman's eyes were missing. In their place, two pools of stygian black stared out from the withered face.

And yet, as Sarah gazed at the woman's face, she had the overwhelming sense that the woman gazed back. There had always been something familiar about that old woman.

Sarah turned away; *leave the horrible thing where it is and forget it.*

She looked around the bare room, with its damp floorboards and moss-covered ceiling. How had her mother lived here alone for so many years?

Sarah was jolted out of her thoughts by the sound of tiny feet pounding down the hallway. A little face peered around the corner of the door and beamed at her. "Hello, Princess Jessie!" said Sarah, "what are you doing making all this noise?"

"This place is big, Mum, but it stinks bad!" Jessie said. "Can I have a look outside?"

"No, sweetheart. Stay inside where Mummy can see you."

"But…"

"Jessie, stay inside. It's not safe in the bush."

"But, Mum…"

"Jessie! Do as you're told," Sarah said, giving her best stern-mother expression.

Jessie stuck her tongue out and pounded down the hallway again. Sarah sighed then returned to the task at hand. She'd given up packing the old, mouldy books properly and had simply piled them in a wooden crate.

There was that smell again. *Something must have died in here.* Something apart from her mother three months ago, that was. She made a mental note to open the windows before they left. Still, there was something more, and Sarah didn't like it.

She read the plaque again. *'Homecoming.'* Sarah shivered. "Jessie!" she called, "Come on, sweetie, we're leaving!"

Jessie's tiny feet sprinted down the hallway. The child crashed into the room and stopped dead, all colour draining from her little face.

"What's wrong, darling?"

"Mum, who's she?" The child whispered.

"Who?"

Jessie pointed past her mother to where the painting hung.

Sarah didn't turn to look, but forced a smile for her daughter as she answered, "It's not a nice picture is it? Not like the ones you make for Mummy."

But Jessie continued to stare at the picture as Sarah began tossing the remaining books in the old crate. "Go and hop in the car, I'll be done in a second." The child didn't need to be told twice, and she scurried out of the room.

Sarah knelt and picked up the crate, her mother's words running through her mind. *We all come home eventually.*

Why was that stuck in her head now? It was almost like she could hear the words, they were so clear.

We all come home eventually.

She froze; she *could* hear the words, as clear as day and as soft as a breeze.

"We all come home eventually… *don't we dear?*"

The crate fell to the floor with a thud as Sarah's strength drained from her body, replaced with an icy chill.

Slowly she turned to face the speaker.

Jessie waited for a long time in the car before the heat of the day finally got too much for her. She pushed open the door and walked across the dried grass to the crumbling house.

She wondered who that strange old lady standing behind her mother had been. She hoped the old lady wasn't still there; she was scary. Jessie had never seen someone without eyes before.

Quietly and cautiously she tip-toed to the room where her mother had been. "Mum!"

No answer.

Jessie poked her head around the door. The room was empty. "Mum?"

There was nothing; only the crate of books, nothing else. No, there *was* something else!

Jessie padded over to the old painting and stared at it..

It showed the front of the house, and there was the old lady she'd seen standing behind her mother. The lady was waving from the porch. Behind her, partially obscured by the painted shadows and framed in one of the house's windows was her mother, her face stretched in a silent scream.

Mrs West's Gift

By Stefan Taylor

When I got sick, our old neighbour, Mrs West, came to me and said, "Don't you worry about a thing, love. I'll help your son off to school. I'll do the cooking and cleaning. You just focus on getting better. Your little boy needs you."

As a single father with a seven year old, I couldn't have thanked her enough. She played with him after school, fed him, and helped with his homework – did everything I couldn't do.

Months passed, I saw numerous doctors and specialists, but all their expertise and tests couldn't change the simple fact that I wasn't getting better.

Then it happened. I went for some routine tests and the doctor gave me only a few weeks left to live. I returned home and broke down.

Mrs West was there of course. She did her best to comfort me. All I could think of was my son, alone in the world. But she smiled kindly and told me to get some rest. All would be well in the morning.

The next day she sent my son off to school, then took me to her grand, old house. She sat me down in the living room. I had never been in this room. It was filled with wonderful antiques and paintings. Just how old was she?

She brought us tea, and for a while we sat in silence. She shifted nervously on her chair. "Michael," she said finally, "I've got something that will help. A gift I want you to have."

I opened my mouth to question her, but she continued before I could speak. She wrung her hands and gestured to a vase that sat above the fireplace. "Can you guess how old that is?"

I confessed that I couldn't.

"That vase belonged to Louie the fifteenth of France."

I frowned. "But that would make it..."

"Two hundred and forty-three years old," she said with a smirk.

I couldn't help but laugh. "Impossible! How did *you* get Louie the fifteenth's vase?"

"The cup you're drinking from," she said calmly, "that was a gift from President Lincoln. I was working for his wife at the time, Mary. Lovely lady."

I shook my head. What the hell was she playing at? And had I allowed this level of crazy near my boy? "Mrs West, I want to thank you for all you've done, but I think it would be best if we don't see you anymore. Especially if you're going to play such stupid jokes."

I moved to stand when she caught me by the arm. There was an earnest look in her eyes, something I had never seen before.

She said, "You may think I'm mad, but believe me when I say that I know secrets others have long forgotten. I am older then you could even dream. And in that time, I have learned many things." I felt an odd flutter in my stomach. "There is a... what should I call it? Procedure? Spell? I can perform. But it will not be easy. You will never die. It is both a blessing and a curse. Trust me, I know. But I can grant you this. You will live to see your son grow. But be warned, if I do this, there is no going back. You *will* live forever."

I stared at her, Trying to find the kindly old lady beneath the crazy woman before me. What kind of sick joke was this? Had she been setting me up to try and con me all this time? Or, was she quite literally insane?

Despite my illness, I found strength through anger. I yelled, swore, called her every name under the sun. Then I tried to stand to leave, but the weakness brought on by my illness had me collapse back into the chair.

She was on me in an instant, her eyes brimming with tears. "Please! You have to believe me. It's true, all of it. I have walked this earth for almost eight hundred years! I was given this gift, and I can only pass it on to someone worthy. Then I can finally *rest*. That person is you. Your son needs you. Let me cast the spell, and then you'll see that everything I'm telling you is the truth."

The burning of my illness lit through my veins, and I thought of my poor boy alone. It is the dying man who grasps at straws, and as I eyed Mrs West, it seemed her truth was carved in her tears. A bark of laughter escaped my throat. This was madness. But what did I have to lose?

"Do it then," I hissed.

With a nod, she began to mumble in strange tongues, and held her hands over me. The room fell dark, as if something had eclipsed the sun. And yet when I looked to the windows, morning light blazed beyond.

A surge of energy coursed through my body. A burning so violent and powerful, I felt I would burst open. I doubled over in pain, gasping for breath, as the energy faded. I felt sicker than ever. All the power drained from my body, and I slumped to the ground.

She was there, holding me, panic and sadness in her eyes. "I don't… I don't think it worked, love," she muttered through growing tears. "I'm so sorry! Forgive me."

Then the light faded and I slipped into death…

I came around feeling that burst of energy surge through my body again. I was alive! It had worked! I felt stronger than ever! The pain was gone. I had to get up and find Mrs West and thank her! My son! I had to find him and—

But something was wrong! The surge of energy was rapidly fading. Replacing it was a burning in my chest, the like of which I had never felt. My eyes flew open, bright lights blinded my vision. I jerked up to sitting.

I made to yell, to call out, but to my horror I found my lips were sealed shut. My cries were muffled, but a scream resounded close by. Something crashed to the ground! My eyes began to adjust to the sterile glow of the lights.

The room I found myself in, was bright and pale. Rows of what looked to be large, steel filing cabinets lined the far wall. Another scream! I spun to the sound and was confronted by a man dressed in a white shirt and grey apron. His horrified glare was fixed on me. At his feet lay a tray of what seemed to be medical instruments. I tried to reach for him, to beg for help, but he turned and fled from the room.

I tried to follow. I called for him to stop! But the movement was agony. I tumbled to the floor and lay there. What was happening? Where was Mrs. West? Where was my son? The pain was subsiding slightly. I pulled myself to standing, shaking my head in a feeble attempt to clear the fog covering my mind. I looked up and froze.

I was standing before one of the huge metal cabinets. My reflection stared back at me in the polished steel. I almost fainted at the sight that greeted me.

My body was cut wide open from my navel to my stomach. My insides were gone! Only bone and bloody flesh hung from the gaping hole.

My lips had been sown shut! My skin was a ghostly white. A small sign on the far wall caught my eye.

It read simply, 'Morgue.'

The realisation hit me, and I slumped to my knees. The spell had worked, but too slowly. Mrs West had succeeded! But, not fast enough. They had thought I was dead! The man had been preparing my body for burial!

The door was thrown open and two men in uniform confronted me. Behind them the man in the apron was pointing wildly. I raised my arms in surrender, tried to beg them for help! But with my mouth sealed, the words were lost in grunts and moans. The two uniformed men exchanged a terrified glance, drew their pistols and fired. Bullets ripped through my already disfigured body, but had no effect at all. I had to get away! I launched myself through a side door, and stumbled through dark hallways. The sound of the men pursuing drove me on.

I crashed through a fire escape and out into the night. I ran and ran, never seeming to tire. Finally, I found myself on a moonlit road far from the city.

I stood alone beneath the lucent moon. I tore the stitches from my lips and howled in fear and confusion. But the sound drifted through the surrounding woods, and fell to silence in the night.

The black woods beckoned to me, so I hurried into the comforting darkness.

I will forgo the details of the many months I spent living in the solitude of the woods. I will not explain how I had to stitch my own body back together. Or the many days I walked in search of my son and Mrs. West.

Eventually I found them, many months after my awakening. They were living happily it seemed, in a small house outside the city. I wanted to rush forward and embrace my son when I saw him, to show him that daddy hadn't left! That I had fought to be with him. But, I didn't dare leave the shadows. He was happy. I didn't want him to see the state I was in. It was clear they knew nothing of what had befallen me. They visited a grave with my name on it, and laid flowers. The authorities had done a good cover up job it seemed.

I followed them for years. My son grew older and so did Mrs. West. One day she was taken to the hospital, and didn't come out. She had finally found the rest she yearned for. My son went to a good family that cared for him, and I returned to the shadows. Soon I lost track of him. It was only once a year on my birthday, that I saw him, when he would come to my grave to place flowers.

He did this year after year. One day he came with a young lady; his wife? Then the next year they came with a child! I wanted so badly to talk to him, to let him know that I was here, that I lived. Well, I use the word, 'lived,' loosely.

Decades passed, and he grew older. I still could not bring myself to confront him and tell him the truth. However, one year, as the day of his visit to my grave drew closer, I decided that I would speak to him. Had it been too long? Had I left it too late? I had to try, for he had grown old now and he was not much longer for this life.

I made my way back to the city, and to the now overgrown cemetery, and waited for him to arrive.

The hours drew on, and he did not show. The hours turned to days, and still he did not come. A hideous realisation settled on me.

I *had* left it too long. My son was dead. I had missed my chance. I returned to my home in the shadows.

That was many, many years ago. I search now for someone to pass this curse on to. I seek out the rest that old Mrs West did. My story seems like it took place ten lifetimes ago. A tale so old, that sometimes I doubt myself in the telling. For places and faces have been forgotten. You may even rightly ask, why I do not give my son's name?

Mrs West was right, I did live to see my son grow. And now, after all these centuries, I can no longer remember his name.

But I still remember Mrs West, and her gift.

Hard Pinch

By Simon J Green

First published at Snap Journal http://snapjournal.com.au

Rick had been on the phone for half an hour. Different voices, different calls, but a solid chunk of time talking through issues with clients and suppliers. At the same time, he was sending off short, sharp emails. He prided himself on his multitasking prowess. Women were meant to be owners of this skill-set, but like all things, Rick had conquered multitasking too, and made it his own. He saw the world as a series of challenges to overcome and make them his. The only reason he hadn't mastered something, was that it hadn't yet been brought to his attention. And his attention was valuable.

Tonight, he'd spent too much of his time answering an email from a graphic designer. He'd looked over the first sentence, glanced at the attachments, dismissed the digital images and flicked an angry email to his marketing manager. The work wasn't good enough, and he didn't have time to explain why. There was better stuff out there in the marketplace. Rick pointed out the original examples he'd shown his marketing manager – the ones from the big firm in town – and demanded those instead.

Why was business so hard for his law firm? He knew they were as good as any of those huge multinationals with skyscrapers in every major city – Melbourne, Sydney, Singapore, New York, London – all those buildings, all those weaselly young men, and yet none of them had the relationships and contacts of *his* firm. The other companies were huge, but Rick and his firm were different. It was not their 'smallness', that word was too weak, it was their *boutique* size that allowed them to forge real connections with their clients.

Rick prided himself on staying awake until 1am so he could call his clients on the other side of the globe. They'd marvel, then joke about the hour he must be facing, and it lit a warm glow inside him every time they acknowledged his dedication. So why couldn't the graphic designer and his marketing manager bloody well see that? It was the third manager Rick had employed in two years. None of them understood his drive or exacting standards. Thus, they either cracked under the pressure or simply left.

The marketing brief was simple: make me what the big boys have. The creatives rabbited on about standing out, being different, and he'd said, "Just make us look big!"

In return, the creatives gave him shit, so he sent the big boys' material across to remind them, again and again, how his firm should be represented. It was infuriating.

Rick sent his last email then hung up on the final call for the morning. *2:30am*. It'd been a long stint. Proud of himself, he shut down his office and pulled on his coat. He opened his phone and, ignoring the weather app he'd never managed to set up, navigated to the weather website. Cold and wet. He'd have to find an umbrella. Switching off his desk lamp, Rick headed to his office door. A small *thump* in the wall above his head stopped him. The silence of the early hours intensified all sound. He paused, waited, heard nothing further, then shrugged.

Rick checked the umbrella stand beside the reception desk, grumbling when he found it empty. Where did the girl keep them? Blast it, what's so hard? He knelt to look underneath the desk. Another *thump* from his office, coupled with three more in the ceiling above reception, made him lift his head and slam it into the underside of the desk. He swore and clutched the stinging part of his skull.

His exclamation seemed to trigger a change in the noise. The thumps became a skittering, like a woman's nails lightly tickling wood. The skittering sound circled above him. He shuddered at the thought of rats in his building. The property manager would get a nasty phone call when Rick returned to work.

As he pushed himself to his feet, he spotted an umbrella lodged under a drawer. It was pink with white spots, and while the colour and pattern would embarrass him, it was big enough to keep his sizeable frame dry. He stood and jabbed the umbrella at the ceiling panels, hoping to frighten the little blighters off. The skittering moved away from him and he nodded in satisfaction.

A large *thump* sounded in his office, followed by the clattering of plastic falling from a height. He peered at his office, unable to see much through the crack in the door. Was it the vent? It sounded like it might be. It was the only thing sitting up that high that could have made that noise. He didn't have photos or illustrations on his walls – they were unnecessary clutter. Desks should only have a single framed item and otherwise be clear. Like the Spartan warriors of old. Remembering his occasional inspiration, he straightened his shoulders and, brandishing the pink polka-dot umbrella, made his way to the door. The skittering was still evident, but now there was an odd, soft dripping noise, too.

Creeping towards the door, he put a trembling hand on the handle and, umbrella held aloft, he pushed. He stumbled back as the door swung open to reveal the source of the skittering: crabs! Scores of crabs, no bigger than his palm and some as small as pebbles, scurried around on the carpet, leaving droplets of water that pooled together in patches. The carpet was most sodden at the wall, where the writhing crustaceans had come cascading from the burst air conditioning vent. Tumbling out the hole, they bounced as they hit the floor then righted themselves before spreading out into the office.

The door he had flung open crushed a collection of crabs. Suddenly a stillness swept through the congregation. Their eyes, little black bulbs, spun on their stalks as if searching for him. Rick stood in the doorway, mouth agape. He was frozen in place by the impossible sight before him. Then as if responding to some universal signal, the crabs charged.

Their pincers – some red, some pink, some orange, some blue – were raised as they rushed him. Rick squealed, looked to his left and right. His brain panicked on a primal level and told him to run, but his body was groggy, slow to move.

A small crab leading the charge, its top carapace faint orange, reached Rick's shoes. Revulsion shuddered through his body, and he turned and ran toward the front door. He heard the thuds and the increased skittering overhead, but refused to acknowledge it until the air conditioner vent in reception fell in front of him. Another huge catch of crabs tumbled out.

This thick knot immediately unfurled and a crab the size of a shih tzu scuttled towards Rick, blocking his path. Rick skidded to a stop, horrified by the ridiculous fact he was caught in a pincer movement by a cult of crabs. He remembered the umbrella in his hand and swung it like a golf club. He ran at the dog-sized crab in the new charge against him, a deep red and bulky creature with a considerably large main claw. With a swiftness and skill from years of strolling the greens with his other fat colleagues, Rick caught the scarlet little beast square in its centre. The crab flew up and crunched into the wall with a heavy crack.

This move, though courageous, left Rick in the midst of the crab's angry comrades. They gripped at his pant legs, refusing to relinquish their hold even as he shook he legs and hopped up and down.

He swung the umbrella wildly, and another large crustacean snagged its claw onto the soft fabric of his weapon. The sudden weight caught Rick by surprise and threw him off balance.

Determined to stay upright, he shifted his left leg to widen his stance, stomping on smaller crabs that cracked and squelched underfoot. He gagged. The initial office wave, led by the small orange charger, now joined ranks with the force from reception.

The swarm quickly surrounded Rick. More and more gripped at his pants. Even as he brushed them off or hit at them, larger crabs used their comrades as foot holds to climb further up his legs, the weight trying to drag him down.

Another deep-red crab gained height, slowly and precisely raising its dominant claw. Rick was preoccupied maintaining his balance whilst trying to shuffle towards the door. A pinch at his inner thigh caught his attention, and before he could fully comprehend it, the sensation changed to a searing pain as his flesh was cut into.

The inner thigh, a natural weak point, sparked off a primitive fire in the lawyer's mind. He dropped the overladen umbrella and swatted furiously at his leg, but the assortment of crabs now draping his pants took advantage. More claws snapped, catching the soft meat between his thumb and forefinger.

Each claw sliced into his flesh. The pain was sporadic at first, and came from clearly identified points around his extremities. Then as more clambered up and found untapped points, the pain began to blur into one great brilliance, burning through him until he let loose a scream.

Those crabs that missed his hands took hold of his sleeves and jacket instead, allowing more to hoist themselves up. The weight was too much now, and Rick dropped to his knees. He could only feel pain. White hot, excruciating pain that no upper-middle-class white man living in the city ever thought would befall him.

They swarmed. Large and small claws hovered up from the mass and pulled at his collar, took hold of his neck, his cheeks. Slicing, squeezing, tearing. His vision began to shift. The insect-like movement of hard chitin caught his eye as they moved toward his face, their furry mouthparts twitching.

Rick's drive, the intensity that kept him barking down the hall at his receptionist, emailing his marketing managers late at night with new instructions; that drive that kept his office chair warm and his wife's bed cold, had bled out of him. He couldn't lift his arms from the weight of the arthropods, let alone fight them off. He was pulled down even further, on his knees and bowing to the carpet of crustaceans.

He could still see from one eye, and became aware, in a detached way, that death was fast approaching. *How could this be happening to me? To* me? Just as he became accustomed to the pain, he felt a shifting and rippling amongst the crabs around him. Their claws tightened even further, snipping nerves and tendons so that a blaze of renewed suffering tore through his body forcing him to jerk suddenly and horribly into alertness.

He felt the flow of crabs from his office swell. Something was pushing them forward. Something was coming.

With a grunt, Rick shifted his head – he had to see.

What emerged from the doorway caused his mind to fracture. An enormous crab, engorged by prolonged feasting, its chrome-black shell covered in sharp thorny spikes. Its swivelling eyes, prominent on their stalks, were like black fistfuls of coal.

Its legs were long and thick like a spider's, and were tucked beneath its bulk. Rick realised the smaller crabs were pushing the monstrous thing forward, scores of the larger ones hoisting from the sides and behind, squirming beneath its body.

They carried the thing out of the office and into reception. The dim downlights revealed where the shining blackness of its shell was broken with red stripes. The colours were dangerous. Rick's body finally voided itself as he felt something deep inside him let go. He was animal now, panicked and frozen with fear.

The ghastly crab finally came within range of its prey. Slowly, the long legs unfurled.

It unfolded its claws, the dominant one nearly the size of its corpulent carapace, the jagged edges of the charcoal pincer sharing the crimson slashes of its body.

Rising up over the mound of human and crabs, it reached out its lesser claw. The smaller crabs dropped off Rick, instinctively making way at his hip. Rick wanted to scream, and oh how he tried when the claw took hold, cutting the already tenderised meat. His eyes rolled backwards, as his mind tried to pull into blessed unconsciousness.

The monster brought its main weapon to bear. The pincer, immense and powerful, hovered in an almost mechanical movement, before opening out around the chest.

Rick's primal instinct for survival kicked in and he jerked awake. His gaze flicked around wildly. His mouth tasted of iron.

The stench of rotten seaweed and earthy faeces assaulted him.

He chortled, blood bubbling over his lips as his mind completely broke. His email had better do the job, or that little prick in marketing was fired!

The claw snapped shut, shattering ribs and carving through organs. Blood burst out over the pincer, drowning the smaller crabs beneath. Rick's upper torso popped up in a heavy narrow arc then fell to the floor.

The crabs moved in to receive their prize, swarming over the meat in a perfect shroud. Small mouthparts slurped up the various types of goo that seeped out. Larger ones sliced up the organs and fat, gathering the pieces to their openings. The gigantic beast dragged the lower half of the body to its fluttering mandibles and sucked out the liver, a much sought after delicacy made sweet by decades of hard living, poor diet and steely determination.

No more than half an hour later, the larger crabs carried their leader out, awkwardly hoisting it up into the ceiling to escape. The tiniest crabs left behind picked and fought over drops of blood in the carpet. Finally, they too shimmied upwards or found alternate escape routes.

In the morning, all the receptionist would find would be two halves of a picked-clean skeleton, strips of clothing, and a ragged pink umbrella.

Deep Stretch

By Simon J Green

"We're already three hours over," Saanvi reminded her client. "I think we have to look at the option of booking me for another half day."

The client, a narrow woman, lowered herself onto her mat. She threaded her arm through her leg and arched them both over her head then looked up at the photographer and smiled. Through gritted teeth, Melody continued pushing the session onward.

"It's just one more pose," she hissed. "Get this and we should be right." As a yoga instructor, Melody had nailed the calm, zenful art of being assertive. It had taken a while – years, in fact. But when someone like this photographer, this *girl* with some equipment and a lip on her, took a tone, Melody wouldn't rise. This kid had no sense of how hard Melody worked. No sense at all.

And Melody had more senses than most. Smell, sight, taste, touch, hearing – ha! She could close her eyes, plug her nose, put muffs over her ears, and yet could reach out to sense the vastness of the universe *with her mind.*

It was during such a meditative state that she had used her powers of perception to realise she needed to build a studio to house her yoga classes. So, turning knowing into action, she sent her need out into the universe. Melody visualised what the studio would look like. She kept communing, knowing in time it would come.

And come it did, in the form of a series of cheques from her father.

Now, she had her studio. The Universe provides.

Melody moved into a variation of the last pose and waited. The photographer stepped back from her camera, arms crossed over her chest. Melody knew what was coming, and while she spoke into the floor, it was loud enough for the photographer to hear her reassurance, "This is just a slightly different version of the last one. I need it as back up."

Saanvi wouldn't move. She opened her mouth to speak, but Melody cut her off. "Just one more, I absolutely promise, then you can go home."

"I have to *pack up* before I go home," Saanvi said, but stepped up and pressed the button, the shutter snapping before Melody was ready.

Melody checked her position and, despite her annoyance at the churlish attitude of this young creative, was secretly thrilled she could stretch her budget this late into the night.

Holding her core tight and feeling a creeping burn up her clenched thighs, Melody visualised her accomplishments. Polished wood floor, enough space to accommodate a session of twenty students. A blackboard feature-wall scrawled in chalk with quotes about positive universal thinking. The reception area was set up to improve both posture and qi, with a desk nestled against the yellow entryway – the colour representing the solar plexus chakra.

The solar plexus chakra was personal power, and this was *her* place, so when someone like this little photographer entered, they did so by entering through Melody's personal power.

Everything was right in this space. Now she needed a set of photos so she could build a website that would capture her perfect poses, her expertise, her *way* to transmit into the broader universe, and help millions grow as she had.

She should call Daddy tomorrow and tell him her new plan.

After ten more snaps, Saanvi immediately unhooked her camera from the tripod and began packing. Melody stood and shook her body out, making loud sighing noises as she released the pent-up energy.

***

Saanvi tried to ignore the stupid sounds coming out of this nightmare of a woman. It was now beyond four hours of overtime. A twelve-hour day, she realised, and for a cut-throat rate in a low-rate yoga studio an hour's drive from home. She was furious, but she wasn't accustomed to venting that fury, so instead her gear caught the rough treatment as it was shoved into her camera bags.

Night had fallen. Melody walked past Saanvi – who was straining as she awkwardly lowered one of the heavy lights Melody had insisted on – and moved to her yellow doorway.

"What do you thiiiink," Melody asked, absently staring at the frame, "about a few quick ones of me at the door, welcoming people?"

The hefty light slid from Saanvi's grip, pushing the stand the rest of the way down in a clattering that left the whole thing vibrating. She checked her equipment was OK, then slowly turned to face her client. "I've already packed the lights and tripod," Saanvi said, pointing to her gear piled nearby.

"But your camera's still out. Just take a few hand-held, I don't mind." Melody closed her eyes, lifted her arm like a leaf caught by the wind, and gently placed it on the doorframe. Eyes still closed, she arched her back, turned her head and hummed through her nose. Melody opened her eyes to find a disgruntled photographer staring at her, camera slung by her hip.

"Ready," Melody gasped between hums.

"Are you serious?" Saanvi frowned.

Melody's eyes narrowed. "Ready."

Saanvi shook her head. She looked at her camera, at the gear, at her car in the street, then finally at her watch. Five hours over now. She boiled inside, a new level of anger that came from hope dashed. She gritted her teeth, took a deep breath and tried to relax. Saanvi lifted her camera to her eye a moment, scoping the shot, then lowered it.

"Can you please try closing your eyes?"

"No," the yoga instructor insisted, "This is the look the

universe wants."

"Please, Miss."

—————

Melody huffed, but acquiesced. She knew she was pushing this kid, but Daddy's cheque only covered one full day of photography, so she had to be a smart business-person in tune with the universe, and compromise. Closing her eyes, Melody waited for the tinny little sounds of the shutter. Instead, she felt a sharp sting in her scalp. She opened her eyes to find Saanvi right in front of her, one arm out near her head.

"What are you doing?" Melody snapped.

Saavni stepped back, lifting the camera as she went. "You had a few stray hairs," she explained, then began taking shots. Melody frowned, but quickly returned to smiling to get those last precious images that would be exquisite on the home page.

When they were finally done, Melody went into the kitchen for a green tea. She left the photographer to keep packing down and loading the gear into her car. It was freezing outside, and the kitchen was furthest from the front door, so Melody stood over the kettle and clutched her hot mug close. She hoped to wait out Saavni, so she could prepare the studio for tomorrow's classes in peace, but when she heard the second ding of her bell and then nothing, Melody knew the girl was inside waiting for her.

"Yes, dear?" Melody queried, stepping into the main room.

Saavni looked at Melody's knees as she spoke. "I'm sorry, Miss, but I have to add a half day to the invoice."

"What? *Why?*" Melody's voice rose dangerously fast through

her grimace.

Saanvi rubbed her arm but pushed on. "It's nearly six hours over, and I need to be paid for that."

"You never mentioned it at the time," Melody retorted.

"No, that's true, but… Well, it's only fair, isn't it?"

"Not at all! I only have so much budget for this, if I have to pay more it throws out a lot of other plans." Melody lowered her mug to the desk and stared at the girl. "This is really unprofessional."

Saanvi lifted her face at that, her eyes suddenly wide, "Excuse me! I should be charging you overtime as well, but I'm just saying you pay me for another half day. That's a good deal, considering—" Saavni cut her words off.

Melody jumped on it, "Considering what?"

Saanvi glowered at her, and Melody threw her hands up, grabbed her mug and turned back to the kitchen. Her voice quavered now, "Send me the invoice, but I'll have to look at my project plans…"

She disappeared into the back room, muttering about being unsure how she'd get the whole thing finished with this terrible shock. In the kitchen, out of sight of the girl, Melody waited and listened. The moment hung, and she gripped her mug. Finally, a stomping and the bell. Melody let out a sigh she didn't realise she'd been holding, and poked her head out. The girl's headlights flashed through her studio for a moment, then swung off, accelerating away. Melody moved swiftly to the door and locked it.

She'd been brave. Daddy would be proud. She was getting good at this business-person thing.

Saanvi was exhausted by the time she got home, but the area she lived in wasn't great, so she diligently took all her gear out of the car, up the flight of steps to her apartment and cached them in the cramped living room. Her anger bubbled as she maintained her usual routine of storing her gear and backing up the day's shooting. She took out her laptop, created an invoice and added the half day.

She sent the invoice via email, highlighting the payment terms of 14 days. Finally, she took a pinch full of long hair out of her pocket, her client's hair, and gently placed them in a small jewellery box on her windowsill. Then she fell into bed and slept for twelve hours.

Ten days later, Saanvi was already checking her bank account and emails with religious fervour. Every time she did, her nerves jangled – an adrenaline dump making her shake as she imagined the upcoming confrontation.

"Please, let me avoid it," she whispered, praying to whoever might listen, thinking of her parents' pantheon and, though she didn't really believe in them, throwing the wish out to whichever set of mystical hands would grab it. This client was into that spiritual stuff… maybe the gods were extra pissed at adherents who failed to be good people.

Fourteen days, the standard terms of trade, came and went. Saanvi heard nothing.

She checked her bank accounts, her emails, and snapped her laptop closed in disgust. In front of her, on the windowsill, was the little jewellery box. An option. The more conventional steps to get what she was owed set her body to shaking – it meant real confrontation. Saanvi looked at her phone; Melody's studio number ready to be called. She looked at the jewellery box. One seemed frustrating, the other a distraction.

Fine. She deserved a distraction before making this horrible phone call.

Ten minutes later, Saanvi was sitting cross-legged on the floor of her living room, surrounded by a circle of red feathers and white clay dust. In front of her, within the circle, was a small figurine with a little base-plate at its feet. Saanvi fiddled with a white, clay shape. The moulding of the clay doll had been the most fun, and she found herself enjoying the creative outlet. *Maybe this is what it's all about: creative release.*

The dust and feathers had been bought online, the jar now sitting on the coffee table, its label in the language of her grandparents. Against the wall beside her was a pan and brush, and her vacuum cleaner, ready to clean up the dust. She may be practicing black magic, but she wasn't an animal.

The clay doll had taken its proper shape. Saanvi opened the little jewellery box in her lap and delicately removed the hair. In one hand was a warm clay doll in the shape of a woman, in her other, pinched between thumb and forefinger, were the plucked hairs of Melody the yoga instructor. After a quick check over the two items, Saavni then stared at the figurine on the floor. It possessed a multitude of arms, all splayed around its body to form a peacock's tail of limbs. Its eyes were cruel slits, its tongue lashing out between rows of sharp, triangular teeth. It looked hungry.

"What the hell am I doing?" Saanvi laughed at herself. She put the hair away, closed the box, placed the clay doll on the coffee table and stood. She felt better. All these rituals probably came from the power of distraction and creativity to relieve stress. Animals cursed with higher thought, trying to outrun fears and concerns. That's why Saanvi took photos: they made her feel more vital.

She nodded to herself, resolving to go out tonight and take photos just for her. She'd clean up after.

Seated at her desk, Saanvi forgot about the dust, feathers and figures behind her, as she dialled the number and held the phone to her ear. She ran sweaty fingers over the points she'd written out in a notebook. As the phone rang, she hoped Melody wouldn't answer; Saanvi had set her phone to private number, and that improved the chances of—

"Namaste, Marvellous Melody Yoga Studio. Melody speaking."

Saanvi's mouth went dry, but she pushed on, "Hello Melody, this is Saanvi, the photographer, I hope I'm not bothering—"

"Look," Melody interrupted. "I'm very busy at the moment. I have a class and—"

"I'm sorry, Miss, it's very quick." Saanvi licked her lips. "Ijust wantedtoknowwhenyouwerethinkingofpayingyourinvoice." She'd blurted it all out so quickly, she worried her words were inscrutable.

"I've looked at my project plans, and I'm afraid I don't have the budget for those extra hours you added."

Nope. She'd heard. And the arsehole wasn't gonna pay. Saanvi looked at her notes, took a quiet breath, remembering all the times other clients had tried to stiff her, and spoke the words she'd written.

"Miss, I'm afraid you have three business days to pay the full invoice before I send the matter to the small business commission. Then *they* can decide what happens next."

There was a pause on the other end. Saanvi's hands were cold and shaking. She knew by the end of that sentence her voice had been quivering jelly, but she'd said it nonetheless.

Melody's voice was low, sharp. "I don't think that's necessary."

This woman was not used to being told no. It gave Saanvi a small boost. "Not if you pay on time, no," Saanvi replied.

The next ten minutes consisted of Melody's various complaints about exploitation, unprofessionalism, how hard it was for her to run a business, punctuated by Saanvi's increasingly bored, "mms" and "hmms." She looked at her notebook, saw she'd covered everything she needed, and jumped in.

"Well, Miss, you said you had a class, so please, three days."

The line went dead.

Saanvi shook from the adrenaline pumping through her system, but she was proud of herself.

On the fifth business day, Saanvi was sick with fury. The email she stared at in her inbox was an insult, and she burned with its impact. A lawyer, *a bloody lawyer*, had sent her a formal letter stating the additional half day was under dispute because it hadn't been clearly communicated, and the client would be seeking official adjudication in the magistrate's court, the fees of which may end up at Saanvi's feet. The real clincher was the surname of the lawyer: it was the same as Melody's. Daddy? Uncle?

Saanvi stood and clenched her hands into fists, pulled them into her chest and growled. It wasn't satisfying enough, so she rushed over to the armchair, grabbed a pillow and screamed into it. Still not enough. She frisbeed it across the room and looked around for something else to do. That's when she spotted the circle. It was still there, the dust, the feathers, even the figurine, right in the middle of the living room.

Saanvi had been busy all week. In all the coming and going, barely home, she must have been stepping around the items, meaning to clean it up but being dragged off to another chore.

She sought out the clay doll, swiped it up and punched it in the head, smooshing it out of shape. She felt better, but then got angry that she should ruin a good little clay doll. She sat in the only space available – the circle – and began fixing the clay head. When it was done, she looked at the jewellery box.

Fuck it.

Saanvi took the hairs out once more and the blondeness of them dragged a horrific image into her head: the vapid, grinning face of Melody, arms and legs above her head, too high up, lifted and pulled so hard that her stupid smile dropped, and she cried out. Grinning maniacally at the image, Saanvi wrapped the hairs around the eyes, chest, crotch, before finally pushing the ends into the forehead of the clay doll with her pinky nail.

She held it above the figurine, the strange statuette with a fan of arms casting a tiny shadow over the surface of its sacrifice plate. Saanvi whispered in her grandparent's language, enjoying the rasping sounds, grunting the glottal stops. It was a good language for anger. She repeated the phrase louder, then a third time. The image in her mind's eye was of Melody's limbs, lifted, pulled too far, the yoga instructor crying out until there was a wet popping.

The violence of her imagination shocked her, and Saanvi's eyes sprung open. The clay doll slipped from her fingers. It fell into the sacrificialplate of the figurine, hitting it dead centre and not shifting, like a magnet drawn to its opposite. Saanvi stared down at it, the lashing tongue and sharp teeth smiling back at her. Did it seem satisfied?

Suddenly embarrassed, her neck flushed with heat, she swiped the whole assemblage across the floor to the dustpan. With sheepish intensity that only added to her sense of unease, she vacuumed and swept and cleaned, then shoved all the furniture back into place, covering up her shameful playing in places she shouldn't be.

Finished, she grabbed her camera. Saanvi had a strong urge to be out of the apartment. The shots she'd last taken for fun turned out pretty good. *Better stick to what I know.* Dashing out of the apartment and down the steps, camera in hand with whatever lens it had on it, she left the rest of her kit up against the wall.

The same wall the figurine now sat against, knocked over on its side, the clay doll still in its plate, still in the exact same spot it had fallen, even though the laws of gravity should have had the doll topple.

The figurine was holding it tight. It had what it hungered for, and it wasn't letting it go.

Not yet.

Not until it had had its fill.

The studio was closed for another day. Melody put the last of the foam rollers against one wall, wiped down and laid out the last yoga mat, and tossed the last towel into the hamper. She was giddy with delight: a full class of twenty to finish the day. The universe was providing. She'd worried that giving the photographer's invoice to Daddy to take care of might put out some bad karma, but after tonight's work, her students were obviously spreading good word of mouth. Her fears were cast aside. Now, a celebratory green tea.

Melody started towards the kitchen when movement out the corner of her eye stopped her. A foam roller had fallen, trundling towards her. She picked it up and plopped it back in place. Cold now, wanting that green tea, Melody paused when the hollow call of her kettle threw her attention back across the room.

Had she started the kettle already? She moved across her studio towards her kitchen, following the sound that was now rising into a bubbling. When she shifted the beaded curtain and poked her head in, the kitchen was still. The kettle sat in its electric base, inert. No movement. No steam. Curious, she crept over to it and, keeping her hands by her side in case of electrical fault, gingerly moved her face over the mouth of the shiny appliance. No steam, no heat, just water. She moved in, could see a faint reflection of the kitchen lights shimmering on the surface of the tiny reservoir just below the mouth.

That's when the kettle clicked on, the light on its handle

sparking awake. In the time it took Melody to move her eye from the mouth to the light, the kettle exploded. Water spouted out, suddenly boiling hot, splashing into her cheekbone and burning deep into layers of flesh. She whipped her head back as the kettle expanded and blew, small shards of metal joining the rush of scalding liquid. The shrapnel crashed against her middle. Fragments cut through the lycra top, embedding in her belly and rib meat. The water scalding the rest, soaking her in pain.

She cried out, slamming against the far pantry, then collapsing to the ground. Her stomach bleeding, her burns steaming, Melody was unable to open her eyes to see the damage. She thought of the phone on her reception desk, and crawled slowly until the beads chattered against her ears, then used the doorframe to pull herself up. She expected shooting pain, but her stomach and chest, while wet and stinging, weren't so bad. She risked touching her belly and found only small pellets of metal that flaked off her skin, superficial wounds at worst. Melody tried opening one eye and found that, while it stung and was fuzzy, her vision wasn't ruined. Confused but sure she needed medical attention, she pushed off the doorway and headed for the phone.

Blurred of vision, squinting, she didn't see the foam roller in the middle of the studio. Her foot came down on the very top of its cylindrical shape. She slipped, her foot whipping out from under her. Melody was horizontal for a moment, like a clown executing a pratfall, then her weight came down right on top of the roller. Her spine arced, the vertebrae separating on one side and crackling together on the other. Her spinal cord stretched to its limits. Melody didn't scream. The feeling was so deeply *wrong* that her only response was for her eyes and mouth to fly wide open, three perfect circles staring up at the ceiling.

She lay there, unaware of the passing of time, frozen by shock. A bright flash of white dragged her back. Melody the yoga instructor had been off in the farthest reaches of the universe, but now, with a second bright flash, she was back in her studio. A third flash made her flinch, and she recognised somewhere in her mind that this was good. That she wasn't completely paralysed. Another flash. Melody lifted her head to see where the light was coming from. In the darkest corner of the studio, a camera on a tripod. She peered at it sitting in the shadows, and as if in response, it flashed again, the brightness dazzling her.

"H-hello?" she called out, her voice a tiny squeak. "I-I think I'm really hurt."

The camera flashed, five shots in a row, like a peal of laughter.

"Please help me," she whimpered, cool tears rolling down her burnt cheeks.

There was a pressure below her waist. Hands, gripping her ankles. She could feel them! And she had enough sensitivity to know they were hands! She wasn't a paraplegic!

"Oh, thank god!" She lifted her head, trying to see over the bulge of her torso. "Can you help me, I need—"

Her legs were yanked, and she cried out. They were yanked again, grinding her injured back over the foam roller. The pain was blinding. The roller now pushed at her shoulder blades, so she was able to see down to her feet, to see who was torturing her.

No one.

The yank once more and a different type of fear overtook her.

"Oh god," she whispered.

Then there were invisible hands all over her. They gripped her wrists, clamped over her ankles, and with incredible speed she was lifted up into the air. She screamed the entire time, from both the pain in her back and fear in her heart. The camera began snapping rapidly, continuously, a strobe light that added disorientation to the terrifying experience.

The hands yanked in different directions and Melody was splayed out, a metre above the floor. Her hands were being pulled to the edges of the ceiling, her feet to edges of the floor, an upright starfish of suffering. She wavered in the air for a moment, screaming, crying, begging the empty space around her, but its only response was to pull. Forever pull.

It heaved at her arms and legs, stretching her, giving her a deeper stretch than she'd ever known possible, an impossible stretch. The immense pressure on her joints grew too great. There was a sickening sucking noise abruptly cut off by wet pops. First one shoulder then her other tore free, until finally and most agonizingly, her legs were ripped out of their hip sockets.

Her scream was savage, wild, and deep. The camera snapped away, peppering her spread-eagled body with photons.

Then Melody, now sensing every small touch, her nerves shrieking in pain but somehow more sensitive in turn, felt more hands grabbing at her. They clamped around her forearms, her upper arms. They squeezed her shins and her thighs.

Then the invisible hands seemed to tense.

The camera's flashing intensified.

"No…" she gasped.

The hands all jerked with hard precision, and every single bone of every single limb was neatly snapped in half. Melody vomited, the hot mess splashing onto the yoga mats below. Her eyes rolled back in her head.

All but the first four hands let go. They began to play, and Melody's arms were swung completely around her body, the biggest hug a human could give itself. Her legs were lifted up past her chest and curved out so that her feet touched the back of head, making her look like a human archery bow. The camera greedily captured these poses.

Those terrible hands kept playing with their toy.

Her right arm and left leg were literally tied into a knot. Her arms and legs were pulled out like two equal symbols. Her feet pulled above her head to where hands might reach, her hands pulled down below her hips to where her feet might stand. All the while, Melody's mind reeled in and out of consciousness, coming back just long enough to feel exquisite pain and perhaps see a foot high above her head or her left hand where her right should be. Then she'd be gone again, no mind equipped to deal with this waking nightmare.

At last the hands returned the yoga instructor to her starfish position. Arms and feet out on all sides like a frozen jumping jack. And they pulled. They pulled and stretched. They dragged towards the walls so that sinew snapped and muscle dispersed.

The tattered lengths of rag that were now Melody's arms and legs were stretched to the point that the skin started to split like deflated white balloons. Blood oozed through those splits, first drops then rivulets that spattered the floor.

The camera's flashes caught and shone in the reflective crimson surfaces that now pooled below Melody. The invisible hands pulled until her left elbow – now a ribbon of red and exposed bone – tore half way through, making the whole shape slouch awkwardly.

The hands stopped their pulling.

The racked and unconscious body of Melody rotated slowly, allowing the camera to snap shots that took in every angle of its subject. Now, with Melody's back to the camera, a hand slapped her across the face.

Melody jolted awake.

She felt everything at once.

Then a sharp twist.

Then nothing.

With her death, the invisible hands let go, and the shredded, broken body of Melody the yoga instructor toppled to the ground.

The camera had vanished.

***

The night air had loosened Saanvi. Her cheeks were tight from cold. Her mind was mellow. The haziness under street lamps had made people walking their dogs appear ethereal. Pink lights from shop windows bled into the fog. The moon was hidden by cloud, so the sky was pitch black. Overall, a fantastic scene to capture with her camera. So caught up in the constant stream of opportunities, she'd forgotten all about the frustration that drove her out of her apartment.

Now she crashed back in, keen to transfer her shots to the laptop and begin adjusting her favourites.

She placed her camera gently on the ground and plopped into her leather office chair. As the computer came awake, she slid the SD card in and waited. Saanvi blew into her cold hands. The little icon popped up on her desktop and she opened the preview window to see all of her bounty.

Her rush was halted.

There were over a thousand files on the card, which was impossible as she hadn't taken more than fifty shots. She scrolled past the photos she recognised, their little thumbnails flickering. When the last regularly named file finished, she saw the cause of the numerical oddity. Row after row of photo files, all named '00000'.

Saanvi scrolled to the first image in this impossible sequence and clicked on it once to view its thumbnail and data information. The thumbnail was white, but she could make out small blurs of yellow: an image far too over-exposed. Her eye flicked down to the data information. Its resolution was right, but the actual data size of the file made no sense.

'0 KB'

Zero kilobytes. That meant it was an empty file, no data at all, yet there was the photo: white and yellow pixels. In an effort to understand, Saanvi tapped the down arrow key and began making her way through the chronology of images. She expanded the size of the thumbnail into a fuller preview, and as she progressed, watched in fascination as the camera found its correct exposure. The flashes illuminated the studio of her reviled and non-compliant client, but Melody the yoga instructor was not in the frame.

Saanvi kept tapping through the mysterious collection, trying to work out how her camera must have accidentally been snapping shots without her realising.

She held down the arrow key, allowing the photos to pass by quickly, like a digital flip book. She lifted her finger when she saw a burst of colour breaking the monotonous view of the studio. Between the shadows of bead curtains, she saw what looked like a small explosion.

I didn't take these…

A chill ran over her. Had she been hacked? Had someone borrowed, or stolen her camera and snuck it back afterwards? That made no sense. She started stabbing the key down again and let the images flow.

Saanvi watched Melody, backlit and difficult to make out, stumble out of the kitchen and cross the studio. A foam roller fell from the wall, untouched, and found its way under her feet. Saanvi gasped when the woman fell, landing at a sickening angle on the roller.

A dark compulsion had taken over Saanvi, a genuine curiosity as to how these photos could exist, mixed with a grim desire to see what happened next.

When Melody began floating in the air, Saanvi's eyes widened, her mouth dropped open in horror, but her finger continued to peck at the key.

The harsh white light of the flash showed the poor woman's agony in luscious, waxy detail, hard shadow thrown behind. In those shadows Saanvi noticed bulges beyond the lines of the woman. Hands? So these were fakes?

Wondering about the software the faker used, Saanvi moved through the images with renewed attention, desperate to spot the trickery.

The sequence in which limbs were snapped and twisted in grotesque shapes, the way blood and bone became evident in such detail, chewed away at Saanvi's surety. The pain, the suffering on display... Deep in her now roiling stomach, Saanvi knew these were real.

She could see the future confirmation. The phone call from the police. Her own guilt driving her to produce the SD card, open the folder to show the officers as some form of confession. The files, of course, would be gone. No hint of them. Just nice shots of winter revellers enjoying an evening. The police would compliment her skills, wave away her fret, tell her she wasn't a suspect, just that they needed to check every lead – Saanvi being out taking photos the night of Melody's death. The passersby who noticed a protruding lens, giving Saanvi an airtight alibi.

The police would leave, one a little concerned and suggesting a visit to a counsellor. Saanvi would nod, her mind's eye fixated on one image she'd not been able to forget since she'd seen it. One image haunting her, day and night, awake or sleeping. One image. The very last in the stream of photos she'd raked through.

One image held, because it was the last and the worst, an image taking up the full laptop screen, its radiation lighting her face.

In the preceding photos, Melody had slowly rotated in mid-air, her elongated and shredded limbs splayed, her back to the flashing camera. Then, that last image, one Saanvi would never escape for the rest of her tormented life.

Melody's head, twisted completely around on top of her body, staring out over her own back, staring at the camera that flashed her final moment of pain and life, neck snapped but her eyes caught in their final moment of perfect consciousness, her eyes staring directly at Saanvi through the screen.

Saanvi slapped the laptop closed so hard it fell off the desk. She stood and pushed backwards in her spasm. The chair caught in the carpet and fell to the floor.

Sudden darkness caused her to look around, terrified and panicked. Her eyes locked on the figurine, still against the far wall, its fan of arms resting it at an angle from the floor, so its sharp smile was askew, its slits of eyes staring at her from across the room.

The clay doll that even now had been locked into its little plate as if it were magnetised, suddenly lost whatever grip held it. The hair-wrapped thing fell to the carpet.

Saanvi screamed.

VISITORS

BY STEFAN TAYLOR

Mitch didn't really want to kill these people. He didn't even know them. Most of them seemed like decent folk, yet every few months his girlfriend, Casey, would get her "hunger."

They'd drive as far from home as they could, finding some isolated house or farm, don their masks and away they'd go.

Mitch looked around the interior of their car; there was blood everywhere – on the steering wheel, the seats, the dash board, his clothes… everywhere. The coppery scent mixed with the musty-dank of the old Holden was making him nauseated.

He wound down the window and sucked in deep breaths of midnight air. Casey seemed unfazed. She, too, was coated in blood. It had matted her frizzy curls together. A large smear beneath her eye, made her look like one of those tribal women he'd seen on

Discovery channel once.

She was humming away happily to herself, the same bloody tune she always hummed; it was driving him nuts. It was all he could do to stop himself from using the Berretta pistol hidden in his jacket, on her. No, he mustn't think like that. He loved her, didn't he?

He was reasonably sure she loved him back; at least she said she did. Sometimes. Although it seemed she only ever wanted to be, how to put it? Intimate? When the couple went out on their little, "excursions."

He'd parked the car on a track off the main highway so they could get intimate, only to realise they were now just a few hundred meters from a large farmhouse. His heart sank. He knew Casey would want one more before they called it a night. She was particularly greedy this evening. And now she was humming that awful tune again. Some stupid kid's song he remembered vaguely from his childhood.

He peered through the foggy windscreen. The only light in the area came from the house.

He turned to Casey and said, "You can't want another one. Haven't you had enough yet?"

"I'm still hungry," she complained, giving him that pout that set his heart to racing.

"Babe, we've done two visits already tonight. I'm tired! I have work in the morning and it's past midnight. By the time we clean all the blood off—"

"Are you angry with me?" Her mood was growing as grim

as the night outside.

"No… I just… this is hard for me, it's…well…"

She stared at him, unmoved. Over the years he'd learned that she was two people. One was the smiling, bouncy girl who greeted him with a kiss and hug when she got home from work. The other was sitting in the car with him now, staring at him with cold, empty eyes.

"Ok, one more," he relented.

Her smile returned.

"But that's it!" he said.

She reached over and stroked his mop of black hair, "Last one, I promise," she said, and returned to humming that damned tune again.

Mitch pulled on his gloves and stepped out of the car. The house sat innocently enough in the distance, light shining warmly from the windows and a faint stream of smoke drifting from the chimney.

He popped the boot, retrieved a double-barrelled sawn-off shotgun, rope and a balaclava. He checked the Beretta tucked into his jacket then headed toward the house. "See you in ten," he called over his shoulder.

Casey continued to hum.

Peter enjoyed nothing more than sitting by the fire with the newspaper while his young daughter sat at his feet drawing a… well, it looked like a giraffe. He'd learned from past experiences not to make any assumptions where his daughter's artwork was concerned.

"Another few minutes and I want everyone at the table please," his wife called from the kitchen door.

"Okay, honey," he called back as he pulled his middle-aged frame from the armchair. Tonight was special; his wife put a lot of effort into these nights. They didn't come around all that often.

"You coming, Elly?"

"In a second, Dad," his daughter said without looking up.

"Hurry please. Mum wants us—"

"But Dad it's *boring*. Can't I just draw, or watch TV or something?"

"You know how important this is to Mum. Come to the table please."

Elly sighed and dropped her marker dramatically before stomping over to the dinner table. Peter smiled; she was a good girl, but it was late, and she was tired. In future he'd try to make these special evenings a little earlier, but that wasn't entirely up to him.

The dining-room table was set with their best china and cutlery. The starter dishes were already there. Bread and butter, mashed potato, a large plate of roast vegetables and meat. Peter couldn't wait to tuck in. As if hearing his thoughts, his wife stuck her head around the kitchen door.

"Don't even think about touching anything until the visitors arrive," she said.

"Smells good, they're going to love it."

"You think so? I've made their favourite, and this time there's dessert."

"I'm sure they will. I just hope we've made enough, they're a hungry lot." Peter turned to his daughter, "What do you think Elly, do we have enough?"

But she didn't respond.

"Elly, what's the matter?"

"Um, Dad…" her attention was fixed on the hallway door.

The *click* of the shotgun's hammer being cocked caused Peter to turn. The man was tall, covered in dried blood, his face hidden behind a faded balaclava.

"Room for two more?" he asked calmly.

———

Mitch had found the family very cooperative. They followed every instruction quickly and quietly, even the kid. Kids were usually the worst, what with their crying and screaming. But not this one, she just sat there, bound to her chair and stared at him. The father was clearly panicking but hiding it well. He and the woman kept exchanging looks, but never once did they attempt any heroics.

When Casey arrived, he'd fix himself a plate of the fantastic spread they'd put on, and sat outside on the porch. He liked to enjoy the night air while Casey did her thing. It was clear they were expecting friends over or something, but that didn't concern him too much. He'd have to make sure they got this over with quickly. Then they could *finally* go home.

Mitch's thoughts were broken by the sound of the woman's sobs. "Look, for what it's worth, I'm sorry," he said. "I don't enjoy this. It's my girlfriend, she gets this urge and well, it's just best to let her satisfy it."

"You don't have to do this," the man said, "If you just go now, we won't tell anyone you were here."

"Ha! You're the second guy to say that tonight." Mitch lent forward and started loading food onto one of the plates.

"Please," the woman this time. "You can't be here, this is a special night!"

"Yeah, well, like I said, I'm sorry but my girlfriend—"

"No, you don't understand," the father said this time. "You can't be here when—"

"Peter!" the woman's sudden outburst made Mitch start.

The man went quiet. Mitch regarded them for a moment. He and Casey had suffered a few close calls before, like the time he'd forgotten to actually tie up one of the victims. The bastard had nearly beaten him to death. Casey had been very upset, said he'd ruined her night. Hell, she'd almost stabbed him herself. He wished she'd hurry up; it had been fifteen minutes since he'd left the car. If she wasn't here in another five—

The front door clicked open and Casey glided in. She was not wearing her mask or her gloves. Mitch sighed; he'd have to remember to wipe down everything before they left. Casey's smile was that of a child's on Christmas morning.

She stood in front of their captives. "I'm sorry if we interrupted your dinner," she said with a giggle before turning her attention to the little girl. "Oh, aren't you precious! What's your name little one?"

The child tilted her head to one side. "Dad, what's wrong with the lady?"

"Eleanor! Quiet!" the father spat.

"It's okay, you don't have to shout at her." Casey stroked the child's hair lovingly.

The little girl looked Casey over. "You're weird," Eleanor declared.

Mitch had to stifle a laugh. Casey turned to him, her gaze cold. "I'll start with her, and I want the mother to watch."

"Okay, but don't take too long,"

Mitch grabbed the father and led him down the hall to one of the bedrooms, closing the door behind them. "Sit on the bed, don't try anything," he said.

Soon Casey would start her little games. There wasn't a man he'd dealt with that hadn't tried some kind of heroics at the sound of his family being... dispatched.

"You really should go," the man said.

"Huh?" Mitch pulled off his mask, didn't really matter if they saw him now.

"I said you and your friend should go."

"Oh, should we? And why's that?"

"Even if I told you why, you wouldn't take it seriously."

The two men regarded each other for a moment. The man was nervous, that much was clear, and why wouldn't he be? But he was treating Mitch and Casey like annoying neighbours who had dropped by uninvited.

He kept glancing out the windows, or subtly checking the clock on the wall.

Mitch put his plate aside. "These friends of yours that are

coming," he pressed the shotgun to the man's head. "How long until they arrive? Don't lie. That would make me very angry. You don't want to make me angry."

The man shrugged. "Truth is, they could be here anytime. We don't know when, we only know the night, but never the time. They just come when they want."

"Well, they better not interrupt Casey. That will make her very upset. And when my girl gets upset, I get upset. Understand?"

The man simply looked away.

"You do realise what's going on here, right?" asked Mitch.

"I know exactly what's going on. But you and your friend don't, which is why you should leave. You're rapidly running out of time."

"Another word out of you and I'll—"

"Shoot me? Fair enough, but don't say we didn't warn you." And with that the man went quiet.

Mitch returned to his food, he was almost relieved when the screams started. The man at least had the courtesy to jump at the shrill sound. "It'll be over soon," Mitch said.

"Oh, I'm not worried about us, son."

For a moment Mitch wasn't sure what the man meant. Then he recognised the scream and sprang to his feet in a panic. "Stay there!"

Mitch bolted from the bedroom and found Casey huddled on the floor clutching her hand. The mother and child were still tied to their chairs. The woman was shaking her head at the child, as if she'd just broken the good china set.

"What the hell happened?" demanded Mitch.

"The little fucker bit me!"

"Fuck's sake, babe, either finish these two off right now or I will! We're running out of time, they've got people coming over—"

"Shut up! I'm nowhere near done with these two." Her fury made him step back. "Besides, it's after midnight! Who has dinner guests coming over at midnight? They're talking shit and you're falling for it."

Casey was up again; she grabbed a carving knife from the table, "Hey, kid," she screamed. "Say goodbye to Mummy!"

Casey brought the knife down hard into the woman's throat. Blood spurted, pumping in rhythmic bursts. The woman's eyes went wide then she slumped forward. Tied to the chair, she was unable to defend herself as Casey continued her frantic attack.

Mitch heard the pounding footsteps of the father as he came running from the bedroom. He turned to face him, raising the shotgun in one smooth movement.

The man raised his bound hands, "No! Stop! You're ruining everything—"

The man's words were silenced by the report of the shotgun. He flew back down the corridor, the force of the impact turning him one hundred and eighty degrees. The man slumped to the floor and groaned.

Mitch stepped forward and fired the remaining round into the man's back. Deep crimson sprayed across the floor. "I told you to stay put."

He turned back to see Casey finishing off the mother. He looked away; this was no good at all. Casey flopped to the floor, exhausted, fresh blood covering the dried blood on her clothes. She grinned at him and opened her mouth, but he cut her off before she could speak. "Look at this shit! Do you know how much work we've got to do to clean this up?"

"Are you angry at me?" Casey said coldly, as she sat up, but he was having none of it.

"I'm fucking pissed!" Now finish the kid, we've got to work fast."

"I want to take my time with her."

"No, Casey. Finish it now or I swear—"

"Ten more minutes," she said stubbornly.

"Five!"

"Ten!"

The little girl burst into laughter, and they spun to glare at her. "What the hell is so funny?" Casey spat.

"This is the best dinner ever," the child beamed. "Nothing this exciting has ever happened before. But, I don't think our visitors will be happy when they get here."

Casey smiled.

"Don't even think about it," Mitch roared. "We don't have time to play anymore! We need to be gone by the time these…these visitors get here."

"No," Casey said firmly. "I'm still hungry and you promised—"

She stopped suddenly, a frown spreading across her face as she pointed behind him. Her finger trembled. "What the… *fuck?*"

Mitch watched as Casey's face turned pale, her eyes now as

wide as saucers. He forced himself to turn. Before him stood the father, two messy wounds dripping with blood and viscera. Mitch dropped the shotgun and staggered back.

The man calmly stepped over the weapon and stopped a few feet from his would-be killers. "Like I said: don't say we didn't warn you."

Casey leapt to her feet and grabbed the Beretta from Mitch's jacket.

The man rolled his eyes. "Sweetheart, if a double-barrelled shotgun at point-blank range didn't do the trick, what makes you think *that* will?"

Casey unloaded the clip.

This time the man remained standing despite the fact his body was filled with bullet holes.

Mitch became aware of movement behind him, and he turned in unison with Casey.

The mother glared at them, her face the very picture of rage.

"How… How?" Mitch stammered.

"We warned you," the woman said. "Just remember that." She looked to her husband, and her face softened. "Peter, would you please clean the table a bit? We'll have to try and salvage what we can from this disaster."

"Of course, love." Peter turned to Mitch and Casey. "As for you two, sit down. Now that you're here you may as well stay," he said as he untied his daughter. "And don't think about escaping, our visitors will be out there by now." He pointed out the window to the pitch black beyond. "Trust me, it's best you meet them in here rather than out there." He smiled as he seated the terrified couple at the table.

The little girl hopped down from her chair and ran to the window.

"What is it Elly?" her father asked.

"They're coming up the drive, Dad. I can see them."

"Finally! Well it won't be the best dinner we've put on, but it'll certainly be memorable." A grin crept over Peter's lips. He gazed down at Mitch, "For *you* at least."

There was a soft knock at the door.

———

When the visitors entered and turned their attention to the two intruders, Mitch felt his sanity run screaming from the room. Warm tears ran down his cheeks, and he may have pissed himself at the overwhelming sense that he would not make it through the night. The creatures were sickly thin, their eyes dark and uncaring. They were so tall, that they had to stoop low to get under the door. Their bony hands stroked Mitch's face, their touch like ice. But the one thing that really disturbed Mitch was their smile. Their mouths were constantly stretched in a death's head grin. Not once did their smile fade either.

At one point he remembered turning to Casey and telling her he loved her, but if she heard, she didn't show it. She was humming that tune again – that damned awful tune – her face pale and distant.

"I know that song!" said Elly, and she began to sing along as Casey hummed. *"If you go down to the woods today, you're sure of a big surprise. If you go down to the woods today, you better go in disguise..."*

As the night progressed, the family talked but the visitors only listened and ate, they never spoke. He felt them probing his mind. Like nails scratching at a locked door. They looked calm, their grins never fading.

Then without warning, the visitors rose from their seats and stalked to the door, waiting.

Peter hoisted Mitch and Casey from their chairs, his grip on their arms like a vice. Mitch wanted to struggle, but there seemed no point. The visitors smiled down as Peter dragged them before the beasts like a sacrificial offering.

"For what it's worth, I'm sorry about this, truly I am. I guess you were just in the wrong place at the wrong time," he said with a shrug.

Mitch tried to back away from the door, but Peter held him firm. "You must go with them, son. You can't go back now."

One of the visitors was already leading Casey into the dark; he could hear her crying through her humming.

"Please...what the hell are they?" Mitch begged, his voice shaking.

"They look scary, huh?" Peter said, raising an eyebrow. "I was terrified when they first showed up, too. I mean Jesus! Look at the size of them! And that smile. But then, we got to know them, and over time we developed a mutual trust, I guess you could call it. They gave us these... abilities, which you saw in action tonight. Then they returned to the bush. But, every now and then they drop by for a little catch up." The old man reached up to pat the thing on its head. The creature bent low to let him. "We make sure no one disturbs them you see," Peter said, gesturing to the bush. "Out there is their home, and we make sure they're left alone."

Peter gently pushed Mitch towards the visitor, "But they don't like intruders, and I'm afraid we can't let you go now. You've seen too much."

"I don't understand!" Mitch whimpered. "Where are they taking us?"

"I think you're about to find out, son," Peter said, "Off you go now."

The Visitor's touch was so cold it burned Mitch's skin. The thing led him out into the night. In the distance, the first hint of dawn glowed on the horizon, but they were heading away from the light.

At one point he called out to Casey, and regretted it immediately. A flash of pain shot through his mind, and the creature grinned down at him.

'Silence!' The word hit him like a punch. He did not speak again.

As he was slowly led through fields and bush, the world grew steadily darker.

Mitch thought he saw shapes dart from behind trees, and eyes that seemed to watch from swaying branches. Somewhere in the distance he heard weeping. He tried to follow the sound, but the Visitor held firm and led him into the night.

Behind him, the morning sun peered over the mountains.

They arrived at the mouth of a cave. The silence of the night was suddenly broken. From deep within the cave, dozens of cold, lifeless voices, echoed up from the blackness. It was a cacophony of despair and terror.

Mitch slumped to his knees, and looked up at the visitor. His eyes were heavy with tears.

The creature's grin never wavered. It wrapped an icy hand about his neck, and dragged him into the blackness. Soon, Mitch's cries were added to the harrowing chorus of voices. The sun rose and the voices faded, to be replaced by the happy chirping of the birds welcoming the morning.

Peter had driven Mitch and Casey's car over to the far side of the house. Now he stood and enjoyed the spectacle of the new day beginning. He let out a satisfied breath and smiled.

He picked up a large can of petrol from the porch, walked over to the car and tipped it over the vehicle. He stood back, drew a flick lighter from his pocket, sparked it and tossed it on the car.

The flames spread hungrily, engulfing the vehicle. Peter's grin spread even wider. He turned and wandered back to the house singing happily as he went.

"If you go down to the woods today, you're sure of a big surprise. If you go down to the woods today, you better go in disguise..."

Trapper Asylum

By Simon J Green

The corridor bore the horrors of misguided humans for over a century. Long since faded were the screams of patients thrown into the antechambers of absolute darkness. Gouges in stone from wrecked hands had been painted over decades ago. The lighting installed to brighten the place now powerless, a tube and its cover hanging solid from webs collecting detritus.

A high voice echoes, suddenly, from around the corner, away from this long abandoned hallway. A girl, not yet nineteen, the colours of her clothes and hair too new – neons unimagined when this asylum was functioning. She stumbles into the corridor against her will, her yelp muted as the weight of the space falls on her.

Leslie's eyes widen as she takes the place in. Her friend enters after Leslie, prodding her. Kylie's colours are brighter still, outshining her friend's. Kylie ignores Leslie's stricken pause and pushes the girl deeper into the hallway.

Leslie turns and slaps Kylie's hands away. It's a sharp strike that catches Kylie off guard. She pulls her smarting hand away, looking at the scratch along her knuckles, frowns.

"You cut me."

Leslie looks at the small wound. Her annoyance crumbles and she steps to her friend, apologises. "I just… this place is too creepy."

Kylie flaps her hand, dismissing the pain and Leslie's whimpering. She steps past her into the faint moonlight struggling through a filthy window. Kylie takes it all in, standing tall, proud of her lack of fear. This is just a stupid old building that'll one day make someone, like her dad, a fortune as a redevelopment site. She turns to the doorways, four of them spaced evenly along the stark old wall.

The first is locked tight, sealed by decades of rust and warp. She runs her hand along the old doorknob and across the flaking paint to the second door. Behind her, still at the corner of the hall, Leslie shuffles a few steps closer. Kylie looks over her shoulder at her frightened friend. She smiles sweetly, beckons. "Coming?"

Leslie peers back toward where they came, as Kylie keeps walking. The lonely darkness behind them is worse than the shared unknown ahead, so Leslie rushes to catch up.

She passes the second door, broken and blocked by furniture, to meet Kylie at the wide open third. Kylie's head is hidden inside the room, just her body and painted fingers holding her against the doorway. Leslie slows her pace, reaches out to tap her friend, then gasps and jumps as Kylie pulls back. Her blonde hair bounces as she laughs at her friend, but Leslie, angry at the taunting, notices her friend's laughter has less volume, less scorn than it might outside.

Kylie steps back and motions with both hands, "After you."

Leslie shakes her head, more angry now than afraid. Kylie recognises the emotional shift and snorts her disappointment, then shrugs and steps through the doorway and out of sight.

Shocked that her friend could be so stupid, Leslie stands frozen at the entryway. Kylie just waltzed straight in, no checking, no thought, nothing. Anger boiling up and overtaking sense, Leslie steps toward the door, then jumps back a second time when Kylie pops her head out.

"I need your phone."

Leslie touches her pocket. "What? Why?"

"It's too dark in here."

"Use your own."

Kylie's eyes narrow as she slaps the door frame. The impact reverberates through the walls, surprising them both. They look at the ceiling shedding dust as the building settles, then look back to each other, their eyes wide.

They burst into soft giggling, the tension of the moment melting away. "Come on," Kylie says. "Stay behind me, we'll explore together."

Leslie switches on her phone's light, right in Kylie's face.

Kylie pulls away, grabs the device, then swings both phone's LED lamps into the darkness.

They're met by boxes and cases, packed high either side of the room, channelling them deeper inside. Leslie stays close, one hand on the small of Kylie's back. Both take in sights through their circles of light, mesmerised by the metal tools and arcane instruments of medicine. Kylie spots something and rushes forward, pulling Leslie with her.

Kylie lifts her phone to something Leslie can't yet make out. Leslie closes the gap, holding her arms as the cool of the room sinks into her exposed flesh. Kylie touches something, pulls back, disgusted.

"It's wet."

"Hang on," Leslie mutters. She steps around Kylie, grabbing a long thin cord. Leslie pulls the cord, and a wide lamp clicks on revealing a table covered in the butchered bodies and blood soaked pelts of small animals. A skinned rabbit hangs from a hook, its viscera fallen into a jar on the table. A fox, fur still on, but belly slit open, is the freshest item under the weak light.

Kylie screams and jumps back. Leslie stares, terrified but silent. Kylie keeps backing away, then stops when she hits something, the jolt causing her to drop one of the phones. She spins. Leslie's gaze slowly breaks away from the meat and bone on the workstation as Kylie lifts her remaining light up and along a bloodied, filthy smock, up and over a hefty man towering above her.

Before the light reaches his face, he knocks the phone from Kylie's hand and crushes it under his boot. Kylie screams. The remaining phone's torch and the lamp light are all that's left, and neither are aimed at the pair. Leslie's screams match Kylie's own. Then Kylie's voice chokes out.

Leslie rips the lamp off the table and rushes to the gargled noises. Determined despite her fear, the weak light reveals an enormous man lifting Kylie off her feet, crushing her throat. His head is wrapped in a hunter's cap, his mouth in a dark bandana. Leslie swings the lamp at his head. The thin tube shatters on impact. The old metal makes a hollow gong sound.

Kylie tumbles to the ground, gasping for air. Leslie grabs her friend and drags her past the stunned trapper.

They tumble into the corridor, now nowhere near as terrifying as what they've left behind. Leslie starts to pull her friend back the way they came, but Kylie's eyes bulge and she falls to the floor. On her hands and knees, she coughs, vomits blood. It spatters out across the floor as she struggles to breathe. Leslie bends to help her when she is yanked by her hair.

The trapper lifts Leslie up. Her skull is on fire as roots tear away. He looks at her, and she only sees deep black eyes so muddy there can't be reason.

They flick to Kylie, coughing on the ground. Casually the trapper throws Leslie behind him, back into his butchery. Leslie crashes into cases in the darkness, seeing glimpses of the trapper as he raises a cleaver and brings it down hard and fast.

Leslie barely registers the sickening thud of steel on bone. She crawls to the small glow of light – the remaining phone. Behind her, out in that dusty hallway, meaty thunks fill the air. No screams, not even gurgles.

Desperate, and on the edge of panic, Leslie scoops up the phone and shines it around. On the table she spots what she needs and yanks a long carving knife out of a fox corpse. She turns to the doorway, partially blocked by the collapsed boxes. There's no sound or sight of the trapper. Leslie places the phone on the floor with the light facing up, then slides it toward the door. The trapper, a hulking shadow, suddenly appears and pounces on the light cast by the phone. He bends to inspect it.

His flank exposed Leslie runs on silent feet, knife out like a joust, and rams it into his side.

The trapper grunts, loud, and swings around, whacking Leslie back. She lets her momentum carry her and leaps away, through the door, back into the hallway. She slips and falls on the innards and meat of her friend. She tries to stand but keeps sliding and falling and squashing insides she can't identify. Unable to process the horror of it all, Leslie begins to cry. Every muscle in her body is urging her to escape. She crawls until she finds dry ground, then lifts herself and runs awkwardly to the corner of the corridor. She barrels into the darkness of the stairwell, her wracked sobs echoing behind her.

She stumbles down the stairs, but keeps her feet enough to crash through the door. The moon sits high in the cloudless night as Leslie runs through the bush that surrounds the asylum. Branches whip at her face, cutting her arms and hands as she charges through the undergrowth. She's not sure where she's going, but knows the hulking shadow of the institute is behind her. Despite her panting, she hears the unmistakable sound of a car speeding past on bitumen. She screams out as she quickens her pace, not paying attention to her footing. The sound of steel snapping. Blinding pain skewers up Leslie's leg, turning her cry for help into a yell of agony. She collapses to the earth and rolls over to see the damage: a fox trap clamped to her ankle, biting deep.

Fevered, adrenalin pumping through her veins, she yanks at the jaws but they don't budge. She sees the trap's chain is fixed with a short steel rod. She pulls the rod out and shoves the steel in to the trap's teeth, crying out again from the bite in her flesh. She clenches her jaw and pushes. Leslie's groans are hoarse from the pain, but she manages to wedge open the trap and pull her ruined ankle out.

A chain rattles.

Leslie pauses and looks back from where she came.

The bushes shake.

He's coming.

Leslie holds the rod, grabs the bloodied trap and hobbles away as fast as she can.

She glances over her shoulder. The hulking shape of the trapper bursts from the bush. Silhouetted in the moonlight, she can see a chain dangling from one of his hands while the other is clamped to the wound in his side, the knife still embedded. He looks around, sees her and takes a step. Leslie flees, ignoring the pain lancing up her leg. She crashes into a small embankment.

Scrambling desperately, she crests it to find a road. She makes it to the road's edge, hears the rattling of chains and turns to see the trapper stomping up the bank. With the last of her energy she lifts the trap and hurls it. He doesn't see it coming. The trap connects with his skull, and he tumbles backwards into the bush.

Leslie staggers onto the middle of the road. She holds the steel rod up, keeping what lurks in the bushes at bay. A passing car slows, someone inside calls out, scared but offering help.

Leslie hears shuffling, the clanking of chains. She squints into the bush-line. The driver puts his hand to Leslie's shoulder and she screams. He ducks away from her swinging steel and calms her enough to help her into the car. In the back seat, Leslie still clutches the rod. She cries wildly, feeling relief but not safety. She watches the good Samaritan step away from the car, looking into the bush, towards the trapper. Leslie calls out, "Please! We have to leave!" and the good Samaritan runs back to the car, gets in and drives off.

The man asks her questions but she can't make them out. Leslie leans over the back seat, looking at the side of the road. She waits for *him* to emerge. Her leg throbs. Pain and exhaustion take over her body. The car turns round a bend and different trees replace the bush-line. Leslie collapses on the seat. Out the window of the car, she sees the asylum. Dark, sprawling, it looks undisturbed. She pictures Kylie's face, hard to separate from the gore that was her friend. It's the last images she remembers before she slips from danger and from consciousness.

THE DARKNESS

BY SIMON J. GREEN & STEFAN TAYLOR

"Bring her here!" Remus demanded. She stood in the entrance of the troop's horsekeeper tent, making way for her soldiers as they dragged in their bound prisoner. Remus coughed as the stench of death hit the back of her throat. It was so strong it was almost a living thing; a mix of blood and smouldering flesh. It suited the incoming captive. Pitch-covered torches mounted in the trees lit up the camp nestled between rocky formations. It also lit dead bodies in horrendous stacks, sharing the border of the camp with the horses. Soldiers dumped more of the rebels' contorted corpses, in clear view of a pen of prisoners. One grim boy amongst the prisoners looked away from the horror, and glared hatefully at Remus.

The commander rubbed her eyes. The sights and smells

made her sick, and the boy unnerved her. She moved to join the soldiers in the tent.

Remus breathed easier as she closed the tent flap and turned to her duties. The troops plonked a chair on the hay-strewn ground. They yanked their prisoner's manacled arms over and behind the back of the battered seat. She was tied down securely. The men stepped back and let their commander through.

Remus eyed the bloodied woman. The prisoner's simple clothes revealed tanned skin, and where there wasn't blood from fresh injuries, a network of scars crossed her body. The scars were the result of dozens of battles fought by blade and arrow. It had been a long time since guns had been used in this war. Remus felt her own scars ache in sympathy. She missed the old days. At least guns could kill quickly. There were barely any left in the empire. The war between the Rebels and the Empire had sucked every resource and industry dry. She couldn't even remember exactly what had sparked the war, or who had been the initial aggressor. Not that it mattered now. All that mattered was ending the bloody conflict and getting home, and now Remus had her chance.

The captive was leaning forward, her black hair plastered to her face and hanging down over her lap. Remus bent to peer beneath, but a shuffling at the entrance took her attention. Two more commanders and their guards stepped in to the now crowded tent. One, a sandy haired man named Morgan, raised his eyebrows at the other, Articus, who was tall and broad. Morgan clasped his hands together above his head triumphantly.

"We caught her!" he declared. Remus stood up straight.

"*I* caught her," she corrected her peer.

Morgan chewed the inside of his cheek, then smiled and stepped to Remus. He clapped her on the shoulder. "Of course, commander," he beamed. "And I daresay, capturing the great death dodger will warrant a ticket home."

Remus pushed his hand away and shot her fellow commanders a dark, reproachful glare. She turned to the prisoner. A pair of crimson eyes peered back. Remus cleared her throat.

"Jorl Arder, I hereby charge you with war crimes against the Empire," Remus stated, her voice cold.

"You will be brought before her imperial majesty and executed. If you answer our questions now, your execution will be merciful and swift."

Jorl smiled a thin, mirthless smile. Remus understood the irony, and knelt down to her prisoner's eye level.

"Miss Arder, I'd simply like to know where you placed your explosive traps." Jorl looked at her captor. The prisoner's smile remained, but now there was a hint of amusement. Remus continued, "I know you've been placing them along the highway. I know only rebel leaders know their location. I now know how to disarm them. I know we will find them, but it will take time. So, tell me where they are now, and make your death easier."

Jorl snorted and leaned back in her chair. "*Leaders,*" she sneered, like the word was a joke. "*They* aren't like that."

Remus' eyes narrowed. "I also know where you were retreating to," the commander continued. Remus turned to the other commanders. "Utopia, isn't it called?"

Morgan nodded, but Articus was busy whispering to his guard. Remus eyed them a moment, then returned to her prisoner. "How *do* you fit so many rebels into such a small town?" she asked in a mocking tone that held no interest in the actual answer.

"When the catapults are ready, we'll turn that small town into a big crater," Morgan chuckled from the corner of the tent. "The days of the great rebellion are coming to an end death dodger." Morgan turned to Articus and laughed, but the tall man grunted and left. Morgan watched him go. Remus shot him a querying look, but Morgan simply shrugged.

Remus pressed her prisoner, "Tell me where the traps are laid and I'll spare the town." Jorl's smile tensed. Remus could see the strain, could see the shift from amusement to a more forced emotion.

Articus suddenly re-entered and finally spoke, his voice low in volume but so deep it carried across the whole space. He held a small boy by the shirt scruff. He waved the child like a doll, as he spoke to Jorl. "This boy says he knows you. Helped lay the traps."

Jorl strained to see the boy. Remus quietly stepped around the tent to take up a position behind the prisoner. As the bass-voiced commander dragged the boy through the throng, Remus unhooked her rapid-fire crossbow from its station and, casually, trained its loaded bolt on Jorl's back.

The boy was thrown down in front of Jorl, his back to her. The child shook beneath the gaze of the commanders and guards. He was scrawny, his eyes large, his hair a bedraggled mess. The sight sparked a memory in Remus' mind.

Her thoughts rocketed over miles and miles until she was

home, with her own son, in desperate need of a bath after playing in the pigpens on their farm. Articus' deep voice brought her back.

"I'm growing impatient," the commander sniffed and drew his blade. He held it to the boy's throat. The child squeaked, his eyes darting around the room, but Remus noticed his hands clutching his stomach. Articus smiled at Jorl as he drew blood. "The location of these pathetic traps or I take off his head."

"Commander!" Remus barked.

Articus waved the knife. "I'm bored with waiting. This rebel bitch either cares about the town, the child, or herself. Let's put an end to all three and move on!"

Remus started to argue but the child squealed, holding his stomach, wincing in pain. Remus noticed Jorl was straining to see his face. The boy turned to both Remus and Jorl. The commander recognised the grim boy from the pen. Jorl's mouth dropped open, her eyes wide. Morgan clapped his hands and grinned at Jorl's reaction, "Looks like she knows him after all!"

The boy raised his head and grinned at Jorl through gritted teeth. "Long live the revolution," he hissed.

He lifted his shirt. A sickening bulge in his belly caught Remus' eye. A great sinking feeling hit her stomach as she realised what it was. She had seen it before. The rebels had sowed an explosive into the child's stomach. The crude stitch work around the device was red and bruised. A black powder leaked out where the stitching had split. The boy slapped his stomach.

The explosion ripped out of the child's middle and sent everyone around him flying away. Jorl flipped back her chair, the base taking the brunt of the blast. She flew back into Remus, who tumbled through the tent's wall to land in a smoking heap on the other side. Her ears rang. Dust and smoke filled the air. She still clutched her crossbow, her knuckles white from the grip. For moments she lay there, until something stirred. Remus forced her eyes open and saw Jorl wrenching burned wood and smouldering rope from her legs and waist.

Both training and a desire to see her home pumped adrenaline through Remus, and the commander rose to her knees. She raised the crossbow to her shoulder and took aim. Jorl was already three, four, five steps away. Another explosion, bigger than the first, threw both women sideways, back into the dirt. Screaming followed and Remus looked around, forgetting her target. Men and women in the same dark clothing as Jorl were pouring out of the rock formations around them. Wounded or simply shell-shocked troops of the empire were being caught unprepared and slaughtered. Behind her, Remus heard Commander Morgan yelling. She turned to his voice high pitched, his left arm was missing. "We're under attack!" he screamed, over and over.

He fled towards the heart of the camp, until a rebel sword plunged through his chest, ending him.

Remus spun back to her prisoner to see Jorl disappear into a fissure in the rock around the camp. Behind her, the empire's troops began mounting a paltry defence. Morgan's words echoed through her mind, *Capturing the death dodger will warrant a ticket home.*

Remus hefted her crossbow, and followed her quarry into the rocks.

The narrow passageway led deep into the mountain. She looked back to see a flood of rebels racing through the camp. Her soldiers were out numbered and unable to escape. It was a rout.

So why was Jorl running? She hurried to catch the death dodger; she wasn't about to let her chance to get home escape. The passageway gradually opened out until Remus stepped into a dark cavern. The weak light from behind lit only the next few feet, but a faint step gave Jorl away. Remus reached into the quiver on her thigh and pulled out a small pitch-hardened stick. She twisted the flint built into a catch, and the stick caught aflame at one end. She tossed the growing yellow flare into the centre of the cave. It caught Jorl trying to wriggle into another crevice. Remus aimed her crossbow.

"Hold it!" she barked. Jorl was dimly cast in the light, but still tried to press into the rock. Remus pulled the trigger. The bolt cut through the air and buried itself halfway into the rock an inch beside Jorl's head. Jorl froze. The next bolt was already loaded in Remus' crossbow.

"The next goes through your eye," the commander growled, and fixed her aim.

With nowhere to go, Jorl stepped forward and raised her still shackled hands above her head. Her face was a crumpled mask of fury.

"Where were you going?" Remus continued questioning her prisoner. Jorl remained still, fury radiating from her scowl. Remus took a step forward and demanded once more, louder. Jorl stayed silent. The commander lowered her voice and asked a third time,

"Where. Were. You. Going?" Before Jorl had a chance to answer, Remus darted forward and drove the heavy wooden stock of the crossbow across the rebel's jaw, rocking her head back. The commander was already three steps back, bow aimed and ready. "If you won't speak, there's no need to keep you."

Jorl smiled, blood dripping over her lip and down her chin. "You need your ticket home."

Remus reached down, and pulled a long, jagged knife from her thigh scabbard, "The empress only wants your head. Everything else is compassion." She shoved the knife away and reasserted her grip on the bow.

"Fine," Jorl snapped. She looked away, into the darkness of the mountain. "A hideaway."

"Why?" Remus pushed. "Your rebels have the camp. They'll welcome their leader's return."

Jorl spat out blood and rubbed at her mouth. "I told you: they aren't like that."

Remus frowned. Again, *"they."* Not *we.* How did these rebels structure themselves? She puzzled for a moment, then asked, "The boy? He meant to kill you, too?"

Jorl nodded and shifted in her manacles. Remus assessed the woman in her crosshairs.

"Then here's the terms," the commander declared. "Lead me to your hideaway, and I'll let you live. Refuse or cross me, and I put a bolt in your heart and take your head."

Jorl shrugged her acceptance. "I'll need my head."

"Good." Remus gave her weapon a small flick. "Lead on."

Jorl began to feel around the cavern. She found the crevice she'd been looking for and melted into it. Remus followed, crossbow aloft. The two warriors pressed on into the bowels of the mountain.

The pair crept through tight gaps that opened to wide caverns and narrowed once more. Remus stayed far enough back to be out of Jorl's reach, but close enough to maintain an easy target. The commander kept her eyes locked on her charge, but struggled to maintain constant vigilance as the stone beneath her feet alternated between crumbling and slippery. After a particularly hazardous route, Remus looked up at Jorl's patient face, only to see something scramble away in the shadows behind the woman. Remus raised her weapon and Jorl ducked.

"Watch it," the rebel hissed. Realising the commander was aiming behind her, Jorl turned to see. There was nothing there. She turned back, the same humoured smile splitting her sweaty face. "Jumping at shadows commander?"

"I saw something," Remus replied, eyes scanning the wall of rock.

Jorl pressed on, chuckling. *"Empire's pride,"* her voice dripped with mock and scorn.

Remus felt in her quiver and touched two more flares. Comforted, she followed her prisoner.

After an hour of walking and clambering, Jorl came to a large door hacked into the rock. She pushed it. The rust held it tight, but there was a hint of give. She stepped back, Remus stepping back in turn, the finger around the crossbow trigger tightening. The rebel lifted her boot and kicked once, twice, then charged the door, leaning against it. The rust squealed in protest but the whole thing swung forward.

Jorl disappeared in before Remus could say anything. The commander rushed forward and burst into the room, her weapon at the ready.

Jorl was a few meters in, facing her guard and smiling.

Remus stiffened, "Do you want to get shot?"

Jorl shrugged and walked off, her manacled hands bouncing on her thighs.

"Don't tempt me death dodger," Remus said, and followed her into the gloom.

The floor was smooth, the space no longer rock but a formed room. Remus sparked a flare and fixed it to a holder on the foregrip of her bow. Hunched shadows wobbled and shifted in the guttering light.

They were walking through the entryway to a shelter.

Guard posts and a smashed checkpoint only highlighted the decimation. Jorl was already at the far end of the room, so Remus jogged to catch up.

"Is this the hideaway?" Remus asked as they passed through a corridor, but Jorl shook her head and pressed on into a second room. Broken desks and small chairs were scattered around. Toys were strewn about. Everything was covered in a thick layer of dust. The commander called out for Jorl to halt. The woman did, watching her guard from beneath her cascade of lank hair. Remus picked up one of the toys, a smooth plastic duck with wheels at its base. She rubbed the grime off to reveal it's bright yellow sheen. Her son had one just like it. Remus looked around and saw the cord that should be attached to the front. She picked it up, but it came away in tacky sections. The cord had been dried stuck in a puddle of blood.

Remus looked up at Jorl, "What happened here?" Jorl stared at the commander, then turned and continued on. Remus dropped the toy and followed.

They passed more schoolrooms, then bunks. Remus was surprised by the size of the place. The Empire had no idea such resources were available to the rebellion. Mountains, forests, even caves were known to the troops that fought at the front line, but this was something else entirely.

Jorl showed no signs that the bunker, and its ghosts, had any effect on her. She stepped over personal trinkets and pushed aside tables and chairs until they came to an expansive, empty mess hall. Furniture had been used to cover the doorway they'd enter, as well as a second at the other end. The other end's makeshift barriers had been torn down long ago. Under the dust, Remus could see long, heavy trails of blood. Bodies had been dragged. She asked again, "Jorl, what happened here?"

As if in answer, a yowl echoed from beyond the mess hall. It was distant, but its effect was chilling. Jorl paused, and then restarted an even, slow pace toward the doorway. Remus followed, the crossbow between them. Another yowl came, and then in response, a series of clicks to Remus' left. Her eyes darted from Jorl's back to the cracked wall. She saw nothing but scarred and broken plasterboard.

Then the flare began to die. Its burn lowered and the light faded. Remus unconsciously closed in on her prisoner.

The light disappeared altogether and Jorl stopped. Remus almost ran into her. She prodded her prisoner in the back with the tip of her bolt. Jorl continued forward.

A scuttling sound, this time from Remus' right, caused the commander to flinch, but her crossbow stayed forward. Another yowl, again from the left. Remus turned her weapon to the darkness. It was all Jorl needed.

She spun her bound hands up in a tight arc, lifting the crossbow high and away. Then her elbow slashed down, catching Remus across the chin. The commander fell heavily backwards, her head smacking the concrete, the crossbow clattering beside her. Jorl pounced on her. Her knees pinned the commander's shoulders to the ground. The manacles' cloth and wire were pushed down over Remus' throat. Jorl leaned with all her weight. Remus strained to reach her crossbow, but Jorl kicked it aside and pushed harder.

A different kind of darkness began to close in on Remus, but within were memories. The toy duck, her son, the pigpen, her husband, and the farm. They were close now. She could even hear the sounds of their dog's nails on the floorboards, running up to greet her when she came home.

A grunt and a scream, echoed from far away.

Suddenly, the restriction was lifted. Air, cold enough to burn, rushed into her lungs. White dots danced in Remus' eyes. Her hands went immediately to her throat. Painful, bruised, but air still clawed its way through.

She rolled to her side and sucked in long breaths. She was aware of the screams behind her, but too dizzy to understand them. She saw her crossbow and wanted it. Dragging herself across the floor on her elbows, she grasped the heavy stock. She took joy in its weight, then swung it around to target her enemy. Between the risers, Remus could see a pink creature the size of a large dog tearing into Jorl. The rebel was fighting back, but with manacled arms and no weapons, the slashing creature was breaking through her defence. The prisoner's grunts turned to screams of pain. Remus squinted. She took air in through her bruised throat and held it. She waited for the gap between the beats of her heart. She squeezed the trigger.

The bolt flew through the dark. The creature squealed once, then slumped on top of Jorl.

Remus dragged herself to her feet. She stalked toward Jorl, loading another bolt as she went. Jorl tossed the carcass aside then lay still. Remus stepped over the woman, crossbow aimed at her heart. Jorl's face and chest had been torn up, blood pulsing from ribbons in her flesh. There was still defiance in her eyes, the whites brighter amidst the crimson.

Remus shook her head in frustration. Home was so far away, the caverns ahead dark. Unknown. But this rebel, this terrorist, this murderer couldn't be trusted to guide her out. Remus took careful aim.

Movement in the shadows caused her and Jorl to look to the darkness. Yowls, clicks and shuffling were suddenly all around them. Remus looked from the darkness back to Jorl.

The rebel's face inscrutable, she glared up at Remus.

Frustration boiling, Remus lowered her weapon. She stepped back and allowed her to stand. Jorl's wounds made her movement tentative.

The yowls approached. Remus pulled the spent flare out of her crossbow and tossed it into the mess hall. She sparked her third and final one, tucking it into the foregrip. Jorl kicked over the beast that had attacked her. They both studied it. Pink, almost translucent skin covered a muscular, squat frame. Its forelimbs were powerful, with huge scooped claws that could both burrow and shred. It had the ugly, blind face of a…

"Moles," Jorl muttered. Remus turned to her, the flare causing shadows to dance over their faces.

"That did all *this*?" the commander motioned to the bunker behind them.

Jorl nodded. "I thought they'd moved on." Beyond the edges of the flare's light, pale, milky eyes circled the pair. "I didn't think…"

Jorl looked at Remus dead in the eye and the words tumbled out, "At the other end of these passages, there's another hideaway. My daughter is there. If you help me get through, I'll take her and leave. I'll never see the Empire or the rebellion again."

The creatures seemed hesitant to attack. Some called over their shoulders, more arriving from cracks in the wall, overturning tables at the two ends of the hall.

The two enemies stared at each other. For Remus, the hatred and distrust pulsed. For Jorl a softening of the edges, but her eyes burned with a desire to survive.

And now Remus understood why.

She burned with the same desire.

Not for herself, but for her *child*. Commander Remus travelled to the far-flung reaches of the Empire not to make war, but to protect her family from it. Remus was not blinkered; she knew the cruelty of the Empire. Her first thought when they'd entered this bunker was that troops like her own had stormed the shelter and slaughtered the children here. Was Jorl's violence the rebel's way of protecting a family under threat?

"What about me?" Remus asked.

Jorl licked her lips. "The rebels have people on the inside. People I still trust. I'll get them to take *your* family, too."

Remus shook her head, "It's just my son. And no, not good enough."

The creatures were in such a tight knit around them now, that the yowls had turned to excited roars.

Circumstance forced an understanding to emerge.

"Fine. I'll…" Jorl hesitated, the words struggling to come. "I'll help you. Both our children leave the Empire, or none of us do."

Remus reached down and plucked the huge knife from her scabbard. She turned to the woman. Jorl extended her bound arms. Remus cut through the fabric and wire. The restraints fell. Jorl rubbed at her worn wrists.

"We *both* have to survive," Remus stated. Her face was tired. The frustration had melted. There was a lot to do. Jorl nodded. She stood straight. The commander took a deep breath, flipped the knife and handed it to the rebel. Jorl spun the blade from hand to hand, getting a feel for its weight. She finally took a firm grip with relish.

Remus spun to the edge of darkness and readied herself, crossbow aimed at a particularly large and ugly brute. Eyes glared at her, pale bodies circled them. She felt Jorl's back against hers. A spread of creatures emerged from the darkness into the light.

Remus fired first.

A bolt flew out. The ugly creature fell dead, caught clean between the eyes. The moles paused in hesitation. With that, Jorl launched forward. The first beast stepped back in surprise and Jorl buried the knife into the side of its neck. She redirected her movement. The knife slid out, a fountain of blood following, but Jorl was already dodging another mole's claws. She bent low, lifted her body, bringing the knife up under the attacker's skull. Jorl vaulted over the creature, bringing the blade tearing up with her. The skin split like an overripe corpse. Remus watched the death dodger, transfixed by her grace. She moved like a dancer in the Empress' court, but drenched in blood.

Remus finished reloading and fired off more shots, the bolts finding new homes in organs and skulls. She kept working through her quiver, her deadly accuracy and Jorl's fluid destruction keeping the moles at bay. The monsters began massing around the rebel in their midst, and soon Remus lost sight of her. Beyond the glow of her flare, the sounds of slashing, grunting and squealing continued, but Remus could not tell where.

Cursing herself, the commander took grim steps forward,

collecting bolts and firing them into the monsters as she went. Between reloads the stock of the crossbow caved in the skulls of those that got too close. They soon understood the lethal weapon and kept their distance.

Remus ran through the hall finding the last of her bolts, then sped to the tables near the far door. Using the furniture as cover, she deployed her arsenal at braver moles leaping from the darkness. Soon it was just her, the biggest brute, and two smaller creatures flanking it, and two bolts in her quiver.

Remus yelled at the beasts and the lieutenants stepped back in fear. The brute pressed on. She dropped her crossbow and held her final two bolts, one in each hand, the tips protruding from the bottoms of her fists. She readied herself behind the table.

The large brute yowled at her. Its lieutenants clicked and lowering their heads. Remus kicked the table. It smashed into a smaller one, but the other two pounced. She twisted, dodged, doing her best to avoid the slashing and biting. She stabbed into flesh, but the wounds were superficial. The brute clawed back and took a rent out of her left arm. Remus cried out, dropping a bolt.

She reached out with her good arm and buried the tip of her bolt into the eye of a lieutenant. Blood sprayed across the group of them, causing a frenzy. Their wild slashing and snapping was the only thing keeping them from organising enough to finish her off. The brute finally pushed through its injured lieutenants. Its gaping mouth reached for her. The disgusting front teeth quivered over Remus' face.

Then blood spewed out of its mouth.

Remus coughed and spluttered, turning away from the warm torrent. The brute fell aside, revealing Jorl, still holding the brutish mole by her knife in the back of its head. She tossed a bounty of crossbow bolts at Remus' chest.

"Come on," was all she said.

Remus gathered herself and reloaded. The last few moles were smaller, nervous. Remus put two down and the rest broke. They scattered away, disappearing into the same cracks and holes they'd entered. Both women were panting from the effort. Jorl's knife arm was covered in the blood of the animals. Remus' face and chest was the same. They looked at each other, the flare starting to fade.

"Still good?" Jorl asked.

"Yes," she replied.

Jorl pointed to the doorway out of the bunker. "There's worse than Moles out there."

"Then there's the Empire."

Jorl shrugged. Remus nodded. Stepping over the corpses of monsters, the rebel and the commander left the mess hall. The flare died and, together, they ventured into the darkness.